LUCY ROSE

BiG ON Plans

by Katy Kelly

ILLUSTRATED BY ADAM REX

Delacorte Press

Published by
Delacorte Press
an imprint of
Random House Children's Books
a division of Random House, Inc.
New York

Text copyright © 2005 by Katy Kelly
Jacket illustration copyright © 2005 by Adam Rex

The trademark Delacorte Press is registered in the U.S. Patent
and Trademark Office and in other countries.

Visit us on the Web! www.randomhouse.com/kids
Educators and librarians, for a variety of teaching tools,
visit us at www.randomhouse.com/teachers

Library of Congress Cataloging-in-Publication Data

Kelly, Katy.
Lucy Rose : big on plans / Katy Kelly.
p. cm.
Summary: Lucy Rose records in her diary her special summer plans—to make a keychain
for her mother, to help decorate the living room, to prevent her parents' divorce, to
vanquish some squirrels, and to enjoy a ninth birthday adventure with her father.
ISBN 0-385-73204-X (trade) — ISBN 0-385-90235-2 (glb)
[1. Summer—Fiction. 2. Family life—Washington (D.C.)—Fiction.
3. Divorce—Fiction. 4. Washington (D.C.)—Fiction. 5. Diaries—Fiction.]
I. Title: Big on plans. II. Title
PZ7.K29637Lr 2005
[Fic]—dc22
2004015279

Printed in the United States of America

June 2005

10 9 8 7 6 5 4 3 2 1

BVG

For Michael Kelly,
my brother, my friend,
my hero, my heart

JUNE

June 1

92 is a lot of days. That is how many we have from the end of 3rd grade which was yesterday until the beginning of 4th grade which is on September 1. I know it is 92 days because I counted them on my Shiralee's Beauty Spot calendar. My grandmother who is named Glamma and lives in Ann Arbor, Michigan, sent it to me in the mail in a big brown envelope that said Lucy Rose Reilly, Queen of Capitol Hill and Washington, D.C., and also had sparkling rose stickers on it. Anybody who is not an absolute infant could tell that I am not a queen, but Glamma likes to act royally and so do I. She got the calendar for free because Shiralee is her sister and also the owner of the Beauty Spot. It came with a card that said: "Dear Lucy Rose, Put your plans on this. Love, Glam. P.S. I already marked one V.I.D. That means Very Important Date."

I wrote a thank-you note that instant because my other grandmother, that is also named Lucy Rose only I call her Madam, says that whenever I get a present I have to write a letter right away that very day if I'm going to have any manners at all. I pay attention to that recommendation because Madam is one who knows an extremely lot about living plus she is the writer of a newspaper column that tells people what to do if they have the kind of kids who won't behave.

Here's what I said: "Dear Glamma. Thank you! I needed a calendar like mad because one thing I am big on is plans even though at this minute I only have 3. Love, Lucy Rose."

One of those plans is to write down what happens in my almost never boring life in this journal that my grandfather who is called Pop gave me for an end-of-school present which I seriously needed because I already filled up the 2 books he gave me last year. When I got this one I said, "Yippee-yi-yo, cowgirl! This book is a beaut."

And it is because it has a swirl design that's the

same as on my cowgirl boots. Plus it's red and they are too.

Here is what Pop said to me: "A beaut for a beaut."

My second plan is to go to Parks & Rec with my greatest friend who is Jonique McBee, and make a lanyard key chain out of Gimp for my mom's birthday that's on July 13 while Jonique makes a pot holder out of stretchy circle things for her mother only she is making hers just for love because Mrs. McBee's birthday doesn't come until January. I do not want to make a pot holder because I have done it before and most of the time just when you are getting finished with the weaving, it pops off of the pokey plastic thing and you can't get it back on no matter what you try. Plus I have never seen one of those pot holders that is not ugly but I am not telling that to Jonique because that would be rude which is one thing I am not.

I wrote PARKS & REC OPENS on the square of Monday, June the 8th, which is the Beauty Spot month for getting Carefree Hair which I already have. July is for Permanent Curls which are another thing I got automatically when I was born. August is when you're supposed to Get Romantic Hair, which I don't have and don't want. It's also where I found giant letters that say: "LUCY ROSE'S 9th BIRTHDAY ADVENTURE WITH DAD!"

That is my top V.I.D. for the whole summer.

June 2

Jonique and I are feeling desperate for it to be June 8. For now, we are 2 girls waiting, mostly at my grandparents' house. I spend a lot of my days and some of my nights at Madam and Pop's because it's 3 blocks away from my house and because my mom has to go to her job which is being an artist at a TV station and because I can't stay with my dad on account of he lives in Ann Arbor, which is where I lived before we got a separation last summer. Staying at Madam and Pop's house is A-OK because it's usually a pretty hilarious place to be.

My mom, who has the name of Lily, agrees with that because she lived there for her whole childhood with her sisters and brother who are all grown-ups now and live far away. My Aunt Marguerite lives so far away her house is in Japan.

Once I asked Pop, "Are you and Madam rich?"

And he said, "Rich in kids."

"My mom and dad are not because I'm the only one they've got," I said.

One extremely excellent thing about my grandparents' house is that there are lots of rooms plus lots of porches and Pop thinks it's fine for kids to climb out the bathroom window and walk across the breezeway roof to pick apricots which is our third big plan once they are ripe. My mom says she gets queasy thinking about it but Pop says not one body has fallen yet and Madam says she needs the apricots.

Another thing about their house is it's old like you can't believe. The ceilings are made of metal called tin that have patterns on them. In my room on my tin ceiling there is a big fan that makes it very breezy and refreshing. My regular room has red walls and a pink dotty bedspread and a mirror that I love like anything that is covered with jewels that are fake but look real and I made it with my mom and not from a kit, either.

The only not-so-hot thing about staying at my grandparents' is that Madam does not believe in cable TV even if it's the kind that is appropriate for kids and she does believe in health so she is big on soybean foods which are not the best tasting but she is also big on desserts which is pleasing to me and to Jonique.

June 3

Here's what happened at my mom's job: One of the other artists had a baby which my mom says is good for the lady and good for us because my mom will make overtime, which means extra work for extra money. "How do you feel about that?" my mom asked me.

"Excellent-O, because I am a fan of money," I said. "How about we use your overtime to buy a DVD player?"

"How about we fix up the living room instead?" she said.

Which I have to say is a good plan because it needs it.

That idea made us go straight to Frager's Hardware store to get paint sample cards, which you're allowed to take home because they are free. We taped them to the living room wall which right now is a color I call tan and my mom calls depressing. My color cards are Sunset which is orange, Caribbean which looks like toothpaste, and Lemon Meringue that is so yellow my mom says it's electric which I say is a big compliment. I also got Raspberry which is jazzy pink, and Conch Shell which is light pink. My mom's colors are 2 greens called Sage and Celery, Periwinkle which is blue, Cream and Ivory which are dull, and Banana Frappe which is actually the color of butter. "We are going to look at them every day until we know which one is the winner," I said.

Then my mom had to go to work so we walked to Constitution Avenue and she kissed me and kept walking to Union Station to get the subway which she says is the greatest thing about city living. I hopped the whole way to Madam and Pop's because I am one person who believes in exercise.

For dinner we had minestrone soup and cheese sandwiches on bread that's called whole grain and takes a lot of chewing but Madam says is good on account of it has fiber.

June 4

This morning I came down the back staircase and found Pop in the kitchen with oat flakes and skimmed milk that Madam left us for breakfast. Here's what I thought: P-U.

Madam wasn't there because she was taking her exercise with a class of ladies. It is not what I call good exercise because mostly they just stretch every which way until they are practically exhausted and have to go drink lattes.

Pop said, "We MUST have something to celebrate."

That's what he always says when he wants

to skip healthy food and go to Jimmy T's which is an extremely excellent restaurant in our neighborhood.

"School's out. That is something to celebrate," I said.

"Good one," Pop said.

Even though he is a grown-up, Pop is not such a big fan of school and he is totally against worksheets.

Before we left Pop said, "Call Melonhead and tell him to meet us at Jimmy T's. We'll pick up Jonique on the way."

Melonhead is Adam Melon. Jonique and I didn't used to like him but now we do most of the time even though he can still get on our last nerves. When I asked him he said, "Sure I'll come. I had one breakfast but I am already hungry again."

There are 2 things Melonhead loves in this world. One is science and the other one is food. The pleasing thing about him is that he is not one to have a panic if things get what my mother calls

OUT OF HAND. Also he is a good sport about being called Melonhead which he says he doesn't mind but Madam says is not thoughtful.

On the walk to Jimmy T's Jonique asked Pop, "Can we have lemonade for breakfast?"

Pop said, "Sure," which I knew he would.

By the time we got there I was meltingly hot so the first thing I did was put my hands on my neck like I was in the desert and say in my completely weakest voice, "Heeellllp meeeee, Mrs. T. I'm starving for lemonade."

At the same exact second Jonique said, "Is Melonhead here yet?"

"Sorry, girls, no lemons. No Melon," Mrs. T said.

Mrs. T is one person who can make you crack up laughing.

Right then Melonhead walked through the door and Mrs. T said, "Well, it looks like we have Melon after all."

"Then I'll have a Melonade," Pop said which had us all laughing our lips off.

We sat at the counter because Jonique and I

are in love with the spinney stools. And when Mrs. T wanted our order Pop said did Mr. T, who is the cooking one of the Ts, make any liver and onions because that is what Jonique loves to eat for breakfast.

"It is not," Jonique said.

Then Pop asked, "Do you have mashed turnips and stewed prunes on the menu?"

"Yes turnips. Yes prunes," Mrs. T said. "They're the special of the day. With pickles on the side."

This set Melonhead off and he started making his hooty laugh and the two ladies that were eating omelets in the front booth popped their heads up to look scowly at him.

Pop is a good kidder but I think he makes Jonique nervous when he acts like that in front of the public at Jimmy T's, so I ordered quick to keep him from getting carried away with himself. "Waffles with spray-on whipped cream, please," I said.

"Excellent choice," Mrs. T said.

Jonique said, "May I have French toast with powdered sugar and two plastic rectangles full of grape jelly for later?"

"Another great pick," Mrs. T said.

"I'll have orange juice, bacon, blueberry pancakes, and eggs over easy, please-y," Melonhead said.

Pop got cheese eggs and scrapple, which is one food that makes Madam feel horrified, and decaf coffee which is the only kind he is allowed to have or he will stay awake all night long. After we made our orders Pop patted his stomach and said, "We are living large," which we were.

While we waited for our food Mrs. T let me and Jonique and Melonhead fill up the metal napkin boxes. She would have let Pop help too but he was filling in the *New York Times* cross words puzzle which is what he has to do every day pretty much first thing. Pop is good at those puzzles because he used to be a newspaperman and he still is a magazine writer. I expect one day I will be good at cross words because I have a quick-thinking mind, according to my mom. Plus, starting this summer I am collecting a huge vocabulary which is the other thing you need. Watching Pop do cross words is how I found out that standing akimbo means standing with your hands on your hips so your elbows poke out and that is a handy thing for me to know because I am one person that stands akimbo a lot of the time. 2 other words that came from the *New York Times* are exuberant which Madam says is exactly the kind of girl I am, and crestfallen which is when a person gets disappointed and their face goes all droopy because of it.

When our food came Pop said to all of us, "What's new?"

I told about needing some plans because of only having key chain making and apricot picking and birthday adventure on my Beauty Spot calendar. "And," I said, "Madam says the apricots won't be ready until the end of July."

"Jonique, do you have any plans?" Pop said.

"Pot holder weaving, family reunion, and a week at vacation Bible school at the Faith Tabernacle church," she said. "And I want to go camping but my mom says she didn't work so hard making our house comfortable just so she could go outside and sleep on dirt."

"Adam, do you have a summer plan?" Pop said.

Melonhead said, "To grow a mustache."

Jonique and I started laughing like 2 hyenas but Pop just said, "Good idea. When do you think you'll start?"

"Soon," Melonhead said. "At least by July."

June 5

I took down the Sunset paint card because it is too crazy and my mom took down Ivory because it is too bland. Then I took down Raspberry because it is too much like my red room and my mom took down Celery the color because it is too much like celery the vegetable.

Later I e-mailed my dad which is a thing I do rather a lot, especially about palindromes, which are another kind of words I have a good way with. Madam and Pop are palindromes because they are the same backwards and forwards. Here's another one: Radar. I learned it from a NO SPEEDING sign. I wrote, "Dear Dad, I think of you morning, NOON, and night. Get it? Love, LR. P.S. I wonder what the big adventure is going to be."

June 6

Today when I got to Jonique's house, her mother, who is one of my best adult friends, hollered, "Come in, Lucy Rose," at me and made a big wave which looked funny because she had her hot glue gun in her hand.

That glue gun is Mrs. McBee's best thing that she loves the most not counting Jonique and Mr. McBee, of course. Jonique was with her in the kitchen and I could see green tissue paper and fake flowers and white baskets all over the table. I was not surprised because Mrs. McBee is one lady that is wild for projects and when she gets going, Jonique usually has to be her assistant. I looked at her right in her eyeballs and said, "What on earth is going on in this kitchen, Mrs. McBee?"

"We're making gift baskets for the seniors that live at the Capitol Hill Home," she said. "I can use your help, Lucy Rose."

"Sign me up!" I told her.

One thing I love to do is work a hot glue gun

but Mrs. McBee is not one for sharing that job. Instead she pointed at the boxes that were on top of the radiator. "You and Jonique take one thing from each box and put it in a basket and arrange everything so it looks perfectly deluxe. And when you're done with one, start another," Mrs. McBee said while she made a glue blob on the front of a basket and stuck on flowers that look like daisies.

"Those are marguerites," I told her. "I know because all the ladies in my family are named after flowers. I have an aunt named Marguerite. Also an aunt Pansy."

Then I asked her, "How come the people at the Capitol Hill Home need baskets?"

"A gift basket can lift a person's spirits," Mrs. McBee said.

"Why do they need to be lifted?" I asked her.

"A lot of the ladies and men at the home are a little lonely. They're retired from their jobs and their kids are grown and a lot of their friends have moved away," Mrs. McBee said.

Jonique and I wanted to help the old people have lifted spirits. So we got to work. When we were done we had 26 baskets filled up.

"I thank you both. I'd have been at it all day without your fine help," Mrs. McBee said.

That gave me a proud feeling. "The baskets are looking extremely gorgeous," I said. "But I have to tell you, Mrs. McBee: I don't think shampoo is such a hot present."

One thing about me is that I tell the truth.

June 7

Tonight I got an e-mail. It said, "Race car. Love, Dad." I thought about that for quite a little while before I figured out that race car is a palindrome.

Then I wrote him back: "RADAR for your RACE CAR."

"That's a great word!" he said.

"I am also collecting a vocabulary," I said.

Then he wrote: "U R GR8."

Then I wrote: "U R 2. How about a birthday adventure hint?"

Here's what he said: "Pack a glamorous outfit."

June 8

FINALLY Parks & Rec opened which I say was about time because Jonique and I were ready to pop from waiting. She came over so early my mom was still in her sleeping shirt but I was dressed in orange spotted shorts and my blue Ann Arbor Aardvarks T-shirt and my red cowgirl boots and my yellow bandana that I don't leave home without. Even though my hair is on the short side I made it go into pigtails so my neck wouldn't roast because of it being 87 degrees outside.

"I have blue-flavored Froot-by-the-Foot for us," Jonique said.

"That is extremely excellent to me because my mom says she will never buy it in this lifetime because of a lot of reasons including that it's blue," I said.

"But I will give you girls juice boxes and hugs," my mom said.

"Thank you," Jonique said. She is one for good manners.

"Is Adam going?" my mom asked us. She does not believe in calling him Melonhead either. I tell her we can't help it.

"Nope. His mom is taking him to the Smithsonian to look at natural history for about the 99th time," I said.

On the walk over Jonique said, "Don't tell Melonhead but I feel shy about going to Parks & Rec."

"I won't tell because I am one who can keep a secret and he is one who can't," I said. "But why are you shy?"

"My dad said we'll meet a lot of new kids," Jonique said.

"Probably," I said.

"Do you think they'll be older?" Jonique said.

"I think some will," I said. "But don't you worry. I'm pretty much never shy on account of me being exuberant."

"That's a great thing about you," she said.

"Plus, when I met you I was a new kid," I told her.

"You are the best new kid I ever met," she said.

Which made me feel delightful.

But when we got there some of the kids WERE older and I was feeling NOT SO exuberant so we just stood there by the swinging gate until this teenager wearing a Parks & Rec T-shirt said, "Hi. I'm one of the counselors. My name is Trip."

Which is one name I never heard of before.

I think he knew that because he said, "Trip is short for triple. My real name is Rayburn Pate the Third. After my dad and his dad."

Jonique and I both think that people who are The Thirds are rich but Trip looks regular. "We are Lucy Rose and Jonique. The Firsts," I said.

"Well, Lucy Rose and Jonique, we've got all kinds of stuff to do here," he said. "How about I show you?"

He told us about Chinese checkers and regular checkers and basketball and pickup sticks and woodworking and crafts and mural painting and kickball and the whole time he was telling us all the girl teenagers were standing around looking at him and acting swoony. That's because he's handsome.

"We're here to weave a pot holder and to make a key chain out of Gimp," I said. "It's called a lanyard."

Here's what he said: "Cool."

The crafts area is under the tallest tree that I think has the name of oak and on the supply table is every color Gimp you can dream of and it comes on spools that are all lined up like a giant pack of Life Savers. "Take your pick," Trip told us.

"My pick is light blue and red," I said.

Trip cut off 2 long Gimp strings and gave them to me. "Do you know how to do a box stitch?" he asked me.

"Nope," I said. "Do you?"

Luckily for me he did know. He put a key clip on 2 loops of Gimp and showed me how to go over and under to make a square and you would not believe how fast he can do it.

"Thanks a mil," I said. "That's short for thanks a million."

"You're welcome a mil," he said back.

He showed Jonique the big plastic box of pot holder loops. She picked light orange and lavender and celery because those are the colors of Mrs. McBee's dream kitchen that she wants to get one day. Then Trip pointed to a girl with yellow hair and a pink shirt who was sitting at the end of the crafts table. "That's Ashley," he said. "She's 9 and she's just moved here."

Jonique and I both made our most gigantic beaming smiles at her and said, "Hi, Ashley."

She gave us a look that was not pleasing to see.

I said, "What are you making?"

"A pink and white double key chain necklace," she said.

"That light color of pink is called Conch Shell," I told her.

"Thanks a lot," she said.

But she said it in a stinky voice.

June 9

Madam is having allergies because of the pollen which gets on her last nerve and makes Pop go

around singing a song called "Summertime and the Living Is Sneezy." He made it up himself.

June 10

First thing this morning my mom took down Periwinkle which she is crazy about but she said it's too much for that room which is not the biggest. "Same with Caribbean," I said.

Then she threw away Cream. "Even though it's a safe choice it would never thrill me," she said.

"Good, because I am one who would like to have thrilling walls," I said.

June 11

When Jonique and I got to Parks & Rec Ashley was already at the crafts table. "I'll sit by you," I said.

"I'm saving that space for somebody else," she said.

"That's okay, I'll sit on your other side," I told her.

"That's saved too," she said.

Which left only 1 chair for 2 people but then a teenager with pierced ears called out, "We have space. Sit at our table."

Ashley looked cranky at that. I don't know why.

We left after lunch because it was so roastingly hot that all we felt like doing was sweating. On the walk to my grandparents' I told Jonique, "I feel sorry for Ashley because she saved those seats for her friends the whole day long. I bet they didn't come because of it being 92 degrees."

"Probably so," Jonique said.

Madam gave us limesicles to help with cooling down and we asked her if she needed help writing her "Dear Lucy Rose" column. She said another day she might. Pop was on the phone telling Uncle Mike about politics which is not a thing I like hearing about so I said, "Let's inspect Madam's closet."

"I'm for that," Jonique said.

The thing about Madam is her foot is puny for a grown-up and the thing about Jonique is her foot is gigantic for a kid. Jonique fits in Madam's shoes which is divine for her because Madam is shoe-crazy and she doesn't care if we try on her shoes as long as we put them back so they match. I picked high heels that are made of light green straps and Jonique tried on shiny black ones. "We should practice walking down the steps because when we're older we'll probably have to do that, especially if we get a date," Jonique said.

We did and that made me have the great idea that we should take a high heel walk to Grubb's drugstore. But by the time we got to A Street, Madam's shoes were flopping off of me. "I can't wait to get big feet," I told Jonique.

It was worth the walking because Eddie the pharmacist told us, "You girls have got more style than New York City."

When I got home I called my dad and told him what Eddie said and my dad told me, "Don't grow up too fast, my girl."

I told him, "Don't you worry. I think I'm going to be short like Mom."

June 13

After breakfast my mom and I looked at all our colors and she said: "It's deciding time. We're buying paint today."

"I am a fan of Sage," I said. "It's like our Ann Arbor family room."

"Yes, but it's too dark for this room," she said and took it down.

Then I did eeny-meenie and Lemon Meringue was going to win but at the last second I said "And you are it" to Conch Shell.

Then we were stuck because we also liked each other's color so we had to think about the sofa we don't have yet and that's when I said, "Banana Frappe is the color for us."

"I think it is," my mom said.

Madam and Pop came over early with paint rollers and a ladder and brushes. "Let the project begin," Pop said.

My job was to put down the drop cloth so paint wouldn't wreck the wood floor. Then Pop got to work painting the ceiling white, which is the only color ceilings come in, I think. My mom gave me my own bucket of shiny white. She painted the high parts of the wood around the windows and I painted the bottoms and then she showed me how to do it so I don't get paint blobs. Madam climbed up the ladder to paint the pocket doors and then my mom painted the wood near the floor that's called baseboard. Pop and I did the window seat which is actually more like a long box under the windows that is completely not comfortable to sit on but opens like a trunk so you can hide things in it. We hide our snow boots.

Then Pop said, "Let's go bananas."

"Bananas Frappe," I said.

And we did. I got a turn with the roller and painted one wall as high as I could reach.

It took all day and some of the night to paint that room but when it was done it was gorgeous like you can't believe. "I feel good being in this room," I said.

Madam said the color gives her the feeling of being relaxed. My mom said, "It makes me feel like this old house is really becoming our home."

Pop said, "It makes me feel hungry."

We were sitting on the drop cloth eating pizza when Madam and my mom figured out that the living room would be even better if it had bookshelves.

"I'll need a nap or two first," Pop said.

I feel excited about that living room even though I have loyalty for our Ann Arbor living room. That means I'm devoted.

June 15

I am what Madam calls at sixes and sevens, which is odd for a person who is 8. Kidding. Sixes and sevens means when a person is not easy about something. Here is what I am not easy about: We have been having the separation from my dad ever since last July and now it is almost this July. Lately I have been thinking that could mean we are really going to get a divorce which is one idea I do not like at all.

June 16

Jonique and I skipped Parks & Rec because of Mrs. McBee needing us to help take the baskets over to the Capitol Hill Home. We rode in their minivan which has a sunroof that opens and cup holders plus a CD player so we could listen to Miss Aretha Franklin who is Mrs. McBee's all-time best singer and is called a DIVA.

We parked in front and Jonique and I carried every basket to the lobby. When she saw them Ms. Bazoo, who is the social director which means she has to be entertaining all the time, clapped her hands. Then she told Mrs. McBee, "I never knew anyone who had such a flair for decorating."

I said, "Ms. Bazoo, if you want to see a flair you should see the McBees' house."

Ms. Bazoo laughed like she thought I was kidding. "I'm serious," I told her. "They have the kind of bathrooms where everything matches and they have little towels for me when I'm a guest and soaps that are carved like swans. Plus freshener that you can spray all over that is called Gardenia. Also their upstairs sink faucet is golden."

"My goodness, Lucy Rose. Let's not talk about my bathrooms," Mrs. McBee said. Then she made me a wink.

Jonique and I made sure the men got the men baskets and the ladies got the lady baskets. "I would be extremely mortified if a man got fingernail polish," I told Jonique.

"Word of the day?" Jonique asked me.

"It means I'd fall over from embarrassment," I told her.

"I would too," she said. "I'd be mortified to pieces."

Here is the thing that made me shocked: Those ladies and men loved those gift baskets. And they were not just doing it to have good manners. Mrs. Flora Hennessy took every single thing out and smelled them and was so happy about getting a bottle of squirting soap and moisture cream. Jonique gave a basket to a man. He didn't say anything but he held it in his lap and smiled.

Going to that home made me feel good in my heart but I am telling you one thing, when I am old I hope people bring me Skittles.

June 17

I wrote my dad an e-mail and told him about our painting job and he said, "Sounds great."

"Have you changed our house?" I asked him.

"No," my dad wrote back.

"Good," I said.

"The kitchen needs painting," he wrote back.

"I want it to be the exact same color," I said.

"Suits me," he said.

"I would not like to go to Ann Arbor one day and see my house totally different," I said. "Not even a little different."

June 18 Countdown: 64 Days

Jonique and I picked up Melonhead straightaway after breakfast but getting him going took quite a little while because he was in the middle of his mustache inspection which he thinks he can see but the truth is it's invisible. "What do you think?" he asked us.

I wondered what Pop would tell him. "Well, it's good you're trying," I said.

When we got to Parks & Rec, Trip said, "Hey, Lucy Rose! How's your lanyard coming along?"

"Slowly, because of having to remember when to make the Gimp go over and when to make it go under," I said.

"How far have you gotten?" he asked me.

"Counting the clip it's not even 3 inches long," I said.

"It takes a while to get the hang of it," he said.

"Pot holders are quicker," Jonique said. "I finished my mom's and one for my granny and one for Madam. Now I'm doing a blue and white one for Lucy Rose's mom."

Which I think is thoughtful in the extreme, even if those pot holders are not the best looking.

Melonhead started his lanyard this morning. It's blue and silver and after about 2 HOURS his box stitch was almost half as long as mine and I have to say, I feel jealous of that key chain.

Ashley came at lunchtime and started working on her key chain, which has a big loop on it so it can hang around her neck and is so cool. I was getting ready to ask her to show me how to make mine like hers when she said, "Do you wear those cowboy boots every single day, Lucy Rose?"

I thought this was a good thing since it showed she was TAKING AN INTEREST and MAKING AN EFFORT, which are 2 things Madam thinks are important. So I said, "Yep. Every day."

She did not say anything.

Then Jonique made the comment of, "It is broilingly hot."

So I said, "We can go put on our bathing suits and squirt each other with the hose in Madam and Pop's yard."

Then I remembered what Madam says about including people so I said, "Ashley, you can come too." And I made a friendly face to show I'm sincere, which means I truly mean it and is my word of the day.

"My aunt has a pool in her backyard. With a sliding board. And I can go to her house anytime I want," Ashley said.

Later when Jonique and Melonhead and I were eating our Froot-by-the-Foot, we didn't share at all.

June 19

My dad e-mailed me: "1 clue 4 U: Bring your baseball bat."

"A baseball bat and a fancy outfit?" I wrote to him.

He messaged back the word "Exactly."
This is odd to me.

June 20

Today I asked Madam, "Can we get a pool with a sliding board in your far backyard?"

She said, "No."

And I said, "How come?"

"Because pools are expensive and keeping them clean is a lot of trouble," she said.

"And we've already got a backyard full of trouble," Pop said. "Madam is having a war with the squirrels and so far the squirrels are winning."

"Why are you against squirrels?" I asked.

"They have a habit of picking our apricots, taking one bite and throwing them on the ground," Madam said. "I don't mind sharing but I do mind waste and this one-bite thing is driving me nuts."

"Clearly, it's time to call in the troops!" Pop said.

I said, "What troops?"

"You and Jonique and Melonhead are the troops," he said.

"Adam," Madam said to remind him about Melonhead's real name.

"I've given up," Pop said. "Those squirrels have been outwitting me since before you were born."

"What is outwitting?" I asked him.

"Whatever I try to do to keep them away they figure out a way around it," he said.

"That is a good word of the day," I told him.

Then I came up with my own outwit. "We should pick those apricots now so the squirrels can't get them," I said.

"That won't work. They're still small and green, and small and green is no good for jam," Madam said.

According to Pop, we need to keep the squirrels away until they are orangeish. The apricots, I mean, not the squirrels.

I gave Madam a hug around her middle. "Don't you worry," I told her. "Jonique and Melonhead and I will think up a plan. And we will save those apricots."

This is a big thing to be in charge of and so far I don't have one shred of a good idea.

June 21

Glamma mailed me a purse made of straw and inside that was a $5 BILL and note that said, "For the big adventure!"

When my mom got home we borrowed Madam and Pop's station wagon and took her overtime money to the lumberyard. We bought so much wood that it has to come by delivery.

June 22 Countdown: 60 Days

Tonight my mom lay down on my bed with me and we looked at the glowing-in-the-dark stars on my ceiling. "Remember I had those in my Ann Arbor room too?" I said.

"Do you miss Ann Arbor?" she asked me.

"Yep," I told her. "Do you?"

"Sometimes," she said.

Maybe that means she is not wanting a divorce.

June 23

The McBee family reunion starts tomorrow in Newport News, Virginia, and it will take the Washington, D.C., McBees at least 5 hours of driving to get there which is why at 7:30 AM in the morning my mom and I walked over to their house to wave them bon voyage, which is the French way to say good trip, according to Madam. When we got there, Mr. McBee was tying the suitcases to the minivan roof because all the room in the back was taken up by Jonique and Mrs. McBee's famous 3-layer sweet potato cakes with pecans and coconut icing. When I saw those cakes I said, "Mrs. McBee, you are a baking diva."

"My mom made 7 cakes and that is 21 layers but really 22 because of the layer that got dropped," Jonique said.

"That is an extremely lot of layers," I said.

Then Mr. McBee told Jonique and her mom, "Hop in, gals. We've got places to go and relatives to see."

Inside the car, every cake had its own cardboard box so it wouldn't get smooshed and the ones that were on the seats were buckled up for safety, just like the McBees.

"I told my parents we could camp out on this trip but they want to stay at Best Western," Jonique said.

"That's still exciting," I said.

"For sure because I get to sleep in a room with some girl cousins including 2 that are teenagers," she said.

"I hope you have the time of your life," I said.

June 24

Our whole living room is stacked with wood and where there's no wood there's Pop's giant saw that is electric. Madam didn't come with him because she had to give a speech to the M.O.T.H.s who are the Moms On The Hill. Even though my mom is a M.O.T.H. she stayed home to help make the bookcases.

"The rule is I'm the only person who is allowed

to saw and when I do we all have to wear safety goggles," Pop said.

"I'm wearing mine even when you're not sawing," I said.

Then he said, "Lily, you do the nailing and Lucy Rose, your job is to squirt wood glue where I show you."

Here is what I have to say about bookcase building: It takes longer than you would think and you have to measure a lot because if you are not exactly exact the whole thing will be crooked. Pop said he learned that the hard way.

By the time Madam came with peach ice cream from Gifford's we were done and delighted. My mom was so delighted she stayed up and painted the shelves white, by herself.

June 25

My dad sent me a letter with a picture of our dog and my dad is holding her paw so it looks like she is waving. I taped that picture on my wall. Now it is one of my best things that I own.

I e-mailed my dad a message that said, "That picture made me LOL." That is a shortcut way to say Laugh Out Loud in e-mail language. Also it's a palindrome.

My mom and I walked to Eastern Market to buy fresh figs for Madam. I am not one for figs unless they are in Newtons but Mrs. Calamaris gave me 5 cherries for free. Madam calls that a little Lagniappe which is New Orleans for getting something extra. You say it like Lan-yap, which I say sounds like Madam and Pop's poodle Gumbo barking.

My mom said, "The shelves are dry so let's get cracking." That means working so we put up all our books plus a statue of a porcupine that was made by me in Pre-K. Then my mom rushed to work and I went to Congress Market with Pop.

June 28

This is the story of last night only I am writing it at 7:30 AM in the morning today. Yesterday one of Pop's cross words was anxiety. Pop says that's the feeling of being a little nervous and a little scared. I say anxiety is a good word for me to know because lately I have it.

I think a lot of the people who write to "Dear Lucy Rose" have anxiety so I figured Madam is probably good at fixing it. I decided to get her to fix mine when I was spending last night. But then we had to get dinner on the table by 6 o'clock sharp because of Pop needing to watch a PBS show about people that live in Peru. Plus I had the job of making salad and I was so busy tearing up lettuce that I forgot about my anxiety until it was night and I could not sleep. That made me have it more. I was going to call my mom but when she's working the overnight shift, she's busy every second making pictures for *Good Sports Starring Jack Denvir* who used to be a famous football player before he was a TV star and Mr. McBee thinks he is the greatest quarterback ever, whatever that means.

I creeped into Madam and Pop's room and climbed up on the footstool and looked at Madam lying in their high-off-the-floor 4-poster bed. I couldn't tell if she was sleeping or just kind of resting in the dark. So I took my fingers and very gently pushed up her eyelids. Then Madam screamed like anything and I screamed from shock and Pop woke up and shouted, "Is someone hurt?"

"My goodness, Lucy Rose! You scared me," Madam said very breathy like.

Then Pop looked at the glowing clock and said, "It's one-thirty-seven in the morning."

Then Gumbo went frantic and took a flying jump up on their bed and landed on Pop's stomach and Pop made the noise of "Onhhggffaa!" and that made Gumbo feel nervous so he started barking his poodle head off and dancing around on top of Madam and getting his legs tangled up in the bedspread and he got dog drool on Madam's head. And Madam made the noise of "Yetch!" And then

Pop turned on the light and everybody was looking at me, even the dog.

"What is it, Lucy Rose?" Madam said.

"I've got anxiety," I told her.

"How long have you had it?" Madam asked me.

"About 4 days or more," I told her.

"Is there a chance your anxiety could wait until the morning?" Madam asked. "I'm better at problem solving when it's light outside."

I thought about that and said, "Well, probably it could."

"Great," Madam said. "We'll talk at breakfast."

"I think my anxiety would be a little better if I slept on the chaise in your room instead of in my bed down the hall," I said.

"That's fine," Madam said.

"Maybe we could all get up and watch a little television?" I said. "That would help with relaxing."

"No," Madam said.

I dragged my quilt to their room and lay down on the chaise and let me tell you, Pop is one person who snores.

Now I am awake and they are asleep but I don't

think it's the best idea to wake them up again so I am lying around writing in this red journal of mine. One thing I am noticing is this book is lasting longer. That is because my letters don't take up so much space now that I am going into 4th grade.

June 28 again but in the afternoon

Madam and Pop were sleeping their heads off until 8:30 AM in the morning but finally they got up and got going, but slowly. Madam is a believer in hygiene so she can't do one thing until she is fresh from a shower and dressed for the day plus she has to put on lipstick because she used to live in New Orleans and no lady that lives in that city would think about going outside with plain lips, so now she has the habit.

After all that we went downstairs and Madam fixed a bowl of berries and Pop got out granola which I love and yogurt which I don't. Then Madam said, "Lucy Rose, how is your anxiety?"

"It comes and goes but it's been coming a lot lately," I said.

"What is it about?" Pop said.

"Divorce," I said. "I think we might be getting one."

"And?" Madam said.

"And that would be P-U," I said. Then I started to cry.

Pop told me to sit by him and I did and he smoothed my hair which is one thing that always makes me feel better. "Your mom and dad have been separated for a long time," he said.

"That's not the same as a divorce," I told him.

"Thinking about divorce is hard," Madam said.

"Hard like you can't believe," I told her.

"Why don't you ask your mom about it?" Pop said.

"I thought of that but then I thought what if she isn't thinking about divorce? I don't want to give her the idea," I said.

"I find that knowing what's going to happen is less scary than guessing what's going to happen," Madam said.

When we were putting our bowls in the dishwasher Madam said, "Lucy Rose, do you want to know what I tell my readers who ask me about how to help their anxiety?"

"Is it talking about my feelings?" I asked her. Because I was not in the mood for that advice.

"I tell them that sometimes the best way to stop worrying about yourself is to help somebody else," she said.

Doubt it.

June 29 Countdown: 53 Days

Jonique got back and came over first thing and brought me a shirt that I love. It says MCBEE FAMILY REUNION on the front.

"Was it fun?" I asked her.

"So much fun because 112 McBees came and about 50 of them were kids," she said.

"Was the Best Western really the best?" I asked her.

"It was a dream. You get an ice bucket in your room and you can take it down the hall to where they have a machine and you can help yourself to all the ice you want," she said.

"Those are the best kind," I told her.

I have a lot of hotel experience from when my dad visits.

June 30

Today Trip showed me how to make my lanyard smooth by pulling the Gimp evenly. "That's bon, Voyage," I told him.

I could tell that he doesn't know French because he just said, "What?"

I had to explain that I was saying, "That's good, Trip."

I worked all the livelong day trying to make that Gimp get flat and was going crazy from frustration. One thing I do not have a flair for is Gimp. Melonhead is done with his lanyard. And Jonique is starting a Gimp bracelet because she is bored of pot holders. Ashley finished her key chain yesterday and she is wearing it today and acting braggy like you can't believe.

Today she didn't talk to us hardly at all except to point at Melonhead and say, "How come he keeps petting his lip?"

JULY

Tonight my dad told me: "Pack a sweatshirt!"

July 2

Jonique and I had a private talk about our 2 lives this morning. I told her about my anxiety and she told me that she feels sorry about it.

Then she told me: "Of everything I ever wanted the thing I want most is to camp and I think I never will get to do it."

"Why do you want to camp so much?" I asked her.

"Because Alexandra Mendelsohn went with Scouts and she said it was so much fun. They cooked chili on a fire and put milk and pudding powder in a balloon and threw it around for a game of catch and it turned into real pudding and they ate it. And they got to brush their teeth and spit on the ground," she said.

"That does sound extremely great," I said.

"What would you do if you were me and you couldn't stand not going camping?" Jonique asked me.

"Beg," I said.

"Really? Usually, you are not a girl that begs," she said.

"Normally I'm totally against it," I said. "Plus my mom is not the kind that begging works on. But you are feeling desperation about this so I think you should try and maybe your mom will feel pity and take you."

We were in the McBees' kitchen drinking chocolate milk out of glitter glasses and eating Marshmallow Fluff on graham crackers that Mrs. McBee made and I told her were as divine as anything. Then Jonique said, "Mom, PLEASE can we go camping?"

"Baby, I can hardly think of something I would enjoy less," Mrs. McBee said.

"But I am feeling desperation," Jonique said.

"I'm truly sorry," Mrs. McBee said.

So I said, "You never know, Mrs. McBee. It could turn out that you love it and the next thing you know it would be your best hobby and you would want to live in a tent all the time."

"Lucy Rose, I love my house. I love my bed. I love my shower. I love my coffeemaker that turns on automatically so hot coffee is waiting for me in the morning," she said. "And I love my daughter. But I am not going camping."

We tried again with Mr. McBee but it turned out he has the same feeling about camping that Mrs. McBee does and even though I think it is good for married people to like and not like the same activities, I think the McBees should try on account of it is Jonique's dream.

Tonight I made this e-mail for "Dear Lucy Rose": "I need to know how to get the McBees to go camping, please."

This is what Madam e-mailed back: "I don't think the answer is to try to change the McBees. Even the best parents can't do everything. Maybe there is someone else who can help you."

I'm not wild for that advice.

July 3 Countdown: 49 Days

My mom and I ate apples with peanut butter for breakfast to give us energy. She needed it to go do yoga with 2 M.O.T.H.s named Jenny and Rhonda and I needed it for Gimp making.

When I got to Jonique's, Mrs. McBee was hanging red, white, and blue triangle flags on the porch roof. July 4th is huge when you live in Washington, D.C., and every holiday is huge if you live in the McBees' house.

"Hello, Mrs. McBee!" I hollered. "Your house is looking extremely delightful!"

"I need a hand with the bunting," she said.

"What's bunting?" I asked her.

She pointed to these swoops of flags that are for hanging on the porch railing.

"Bunting is a great word of the day," I said.

By the time Jonique came out, there was an Uncle Sam in the yard that counting his hat was as tall as Mr. McBee. Jonique said, "My dad cut him out of wood and my mom painted him," she said.

That yard was so gorgeous I almost felt like skipping Parks & Rec just to see what would happen next.

The 4th of July

This is the day that everybody on Capitol Hill goes to the Capitol. We went early because I will tell you, those sidewalks get crowded like you wouldn't believe. There were slowpokes and fastpokes and strollers with babies and everybody was walking the same way so it was like a traffic jam made of people. Pop carried a basket of Madam's holiday chicken plus red beans and rice like she ate when she was a kid and still eats now. Madam brought a quilt that's too raggedy to go on a bed. My mom had a sack with cherry pie and spinach salad. I had to carry 2 bottles of fizzy water which was extremely exhausting for my arms.

Our plan was to meet the McBees near the

Capitol steps but there were so many people that I was feeling trapped by arms and legs until Pop lifted me up onto his shoulders. "You're the look-out. So look until you find them," he said.

I stared at all those people and then I called out, "Ahoy there, Mrs. McBee!"

She was holding red, white, and blue balloons and was wearing a Statue of Liberty crown made of green sponges. "Ahoy yourself, Lucy Rose," she said and bobbled her balloons at me.

"Come this way," I told her. "Madam put the quilt out."

The McBees put their fuzzy red blanket so it was touching ours. "I told the Melons to look for balloons," Mrs. McBee said.

"That is one smartie idea, I must say," I told her.

"I'm not the only one that thought of it," Mrs. McBee said.

The Melons found our balloons and us and then we had 3 families on 3 blankets and we all shared food and the best thing was Mrs. McBee's flag cake that had strawberry stripes and blueberries for stars and my best thing that is Cool Whip.

By the time we finished dinner the land around the Capitol was filled with so many people and so many picnics that you could not see one dot of grass. Then the "Star Spangled Banner" started and everybody stood up and sang and I think my singing was the loudest of all. Pop thinks so too.

When it got dark they shot the fireworks off over the Washington Monument and every time they did one Jonique and I would say "Ooo-aaahhh" at the same exact time. I'll tell you this about those fireworks: They are a spectacle, which means they are amazing to look at and is my word for today.

July 5

When I got home this afternoon I called my dad. Once he knew it was me he said, "Hey, hey! What do you say?" which is a song at Camp Timberline, where he works when school's out.

"I say, I GOT A JOB! JONIQUE DID TOO!" I shouted.

"That's great! Tell me all about it!" he said.

"It is not the kind that pays. We are Bingo callers. Mrs. McBee set it up with Ms. Bazoo. So from now on as long as it's summer we go to the Capitol Hill Home one time every week."

"What day do you work?" my dad said.

"Different days but always at 1 o'clock PM," I said. "I wrote which ones on my Beauty Spot calendar."

"When do you start and what do you do?" he asked me.

"Today was our first day. We have to spin a silver cage full of balls and when one pops out we read the letter and number that are on it. The biggest thing is to be loud because a lot of the retired have bad hearing. Since I am the loudest I did the announcing and Jonique did the spinning."

"Is it hard?" my dad asked me.

"No. They have a microphone. But it is important to wait the right amount of time for people to find their numbers but not too long or Mrs. Hennessy will tell us to 'Get going,' " I said.

"Is she a grouch?" my dad asked me.

"Nope. According to Madam, she's a pip, which is actually a palindrome," I said.

"Good one," my dad said. "But why is she a pip?"

"Because whenever I call out 'B-4' she hollers 'NOT AFTER!' Then Mrs. Zuckerman gives her a very tired look. Also, sometimes Mrs. Hennessy calls 'BINGO' when she doesn't have it. Then Mrs. Zuckerman feels testy with her and Mrs. Hennessy says, 'Just kidding!' and she laughs. But Mrs. Zuckerman does not. She is serious about Bingo because we give out prizes and she likes to win a free manicure at House of Nails," I said.

"It sounds like there are a lot of personalities at the Capitol Hill Home," my dad said.

"Good personalities," I said. "Mr. Emanuel Woods is one plus he's generous because when he won a bag of spearmint gumdrops he passed them all around and when it got to me and Jonique he said, 'Take 2. They're small.' So we did. But when it was her turn Mrs. Hennessy said, 'They are VERY small.' Then she took 4."

"Wow!" he said.

"Palindrome again," I said even though he already knew it.

"Who else do you like?" he asked me.

"Mrs. Hennessy. I don't think she remembers us from when we came before but I am a fan of her attitude. I like her jokes plus she is cheery even when she loses her pocketbook or her glasses or her keys to her apartment upstairs. That happens kind of a lot because she puts them down every 5 minutes and when she can't find them she tells Ms. Bazoo that maybe Mrs. Zuckerman took them and Ms. Bazoo says she did not and then she finds them for her, usually on the couch. Some of the ladies at the Capitol Hill Home pin their keys to their dresses but Mrs. Hennessy won't do it because she says it would make her look like an old bat."

Then my dad said: "Lucy Rose. I am so proud of you."

"I am proud of myself, too," I said.

July 6

The first thing that came in my brain today was an apricot-saving idea. I got Jonique and we went to Melonhead's and I said, "We need your boom box."

He put it in his wagon and we pulled it over to Madam and Pop's and carried it upstairs and climbed out my bedroom window to the porch, which is a good place to get a view of the apricot tree. Madam and Pop climbed out after us, which I expected because the thing about them is they always have a lot of curiosity about what we're doing.

Melonhead put the boom box on the railing and shouted in his loudest voice, "Listen up, squirrels!"

Jonique put in my CD of *Oklahoma!* and played "Surrey with the Fringe on Top" as loud as it would go. I sang along at the tip-top of my lungs because I am wild for Broadway music and especially that song, which even though it is extremely pleasing to people, I thought would sound scary to squirrels and it must because they all went running right over the fence into Mrs. Napper's yard. Also the pigeons flew away which Madam said was an added bonus. I kept singing and the squirrels stayed away but Mrs. Napper did not. It turns out she is not too hot for show tunes and I said, "Even 'Don't Cry for Me Argentina'?" and she said yes even that.

"It was a great try," Madam said.

"It was some of the most original thinking I have ever seen," Pop said.

But that night, when my mom and I were sitting on our porch swing eating ice cream sandwiches that we made ourselves, I told her, "Original or not, our plan was a dud."

Which, I pointed out, is a palindrome.

July 7

My mom is working a double shift but it didn't start until afternoon so this morning she said, "Girls' outing!" and we got Madam and went to the flea market which has every kind of thing except fleas. "Look at this great clown picture," I said.

"I don't think it's meant for us," my mom said.

What was meant for us was a coffee table that has curling metal legs and a glass top that I thought cost a lot but my mom said was a big bargain.

Madam bought the living room a present which is a washtub that is made of copper which is the same metal they make pennies out of. It is from before they invented washing machines and people had to scrub their clothes in puny tubs which I think would be fun the first time but not after that. We're going to shine it and keep our newspapers in it.

Now the table and the washtub are in our living room with the books on the shelves but to tell you the truth they look a little lonely.

July 8

Here's the thing that made me steaming: We were at the crafts table and Melonhead said, "Hey, look at this, Jonique."

He was pointing at his lip and I got a sickening feeling.

"Look at what?" Ashley asked him.

"My mustache," Melonhead said.

"Your what?" Ashley said, getting so close that her eyeballs were about 2 inches away from his nostrils.

I could tell that this was not going to be good so I jumped up and said, "Come on, Melonhead, we've got to go home." And I made my URGENT look at him which means it is practically an EMERGENCY and he should PAY ATTENTION.

But he blurted it right out: "I'm growing a mustache."

Ashley started laughing so hard that her braids were flapping. Then she called over to all the 13-year-old girls who were at the games table, "He says he's growing a mustache."

Those girls came over and looked at Melonhead up close and Ashley said, "I must need glasses because I can't see it."

Then all those girls started laughing like Ashley was funnier than a TV show. I felt wild with anger, and I looked at Jonique and I could tell she was feeling the same. When I looked at Melonhead I could tell that he was about to cry. So I did the only thing I could think of. I grabbed his hand and Jonique's so we could leave but before we did I looked right at Ashley and I said, "You are one big irrigation to me!"

We left but I could hear a lot of laughing behind us.

"You told that girl," Jonique said. "But what is irrigation?"

"I meant to say irritation but I was so mad it came out wrong," I said.

"Irrigation is a machine made of pipes that farmers use to water their fields," Melonhead said.

At least it made him laugh.

July 9

Instead of eating lunch my mom went to a store and bought a living room rug that Pop had to drive over and pick up. It's yellow and according to Madam it has style.

July 10 Countdown: 42 Days

I called my dad. "News flash! I finished making the key chain that's for Mom's birthday that's in 3 DAYS."

I told him that for a reminder and for a hint.

"I'm sure she will love it," he said.

"I hope," I told him.

But I was really wishing he would say he was sending a present for her.

July 11

When my dad called today I asked him, "Do you remember when you gave Mom those dangling earrings for her birthday?"

"I remember," he said.

"She loves them," I said. "She says you have good taste."

"Glad to hear it because last Saturday I went shopping for your birthday," he said.

Which was not the birthday I wanted to talk about.

Then my dad said, "Lucy Rose, I have the feeling you think I should send Mom a birthday present."

"I do have that feeling exactly," I told him. "It's a V.I.D."

"I don't think Mom expects a present from me," he said.

"Which is why it would be a great surprise," I told him.

"I mailed her a card," he said.

"I hope it's a fancy one," I said.

I feel like I'm exasperated with him. Pop says that is when you are at your wits' end. It's also my word of the day.

July 12

I skipped Parks & Rec, which was A-OK with me because I was not in the mood to see Ashley. My mom needed me to help make cold tomato soup called gazpacho which sounds P-U but is actually good, if you like tomatoes, which I do except for stewed. Madam came over to eat soup and stayed to drink tea with my mom so I got Jonique and Melonhead and we walked to Grubb's and had a big chat with Eddie about his daughter that is an actress and also a waitress. Then we used my quarter and Melonhead's nickel and Jonique's 37 cents to buy Lemonheads. They are not the best but they do last a long time plus we couldn't agree on any other candy. "They'd be better if they were called Melonheads," I said.

That made Jonique laugh and Melonhead wish it was true.

We sat outside on the bench and divided them up so Melonhead and I got 9 each and Jonique got 10 on account of she had given the most money. Before I put the first Lemonhead in my mouth I looked at both of them and said, "I am famished like you wouldn't believe."

"That means hungry," Jonique told Melonhead. "It's her word of the day."

"Big whup," Melonhead said.

Sometimes he is not what you would call thoughtful.

July 13

I spent the whole day at Madam and Pop's cooking osso buco for my mom's birthday because it is her favorite. It is mostly made of bones, which sounds disgusting but tastes good on account of there's some meat on them and they have a sauce. Then we made a lemon cake that's my favorite and covered it with white icing plus a whole box of candles. While we were doing that, Pop and Gumbo went to the store to buy the kind of balloons that float automatically and a huge lot of lilies.

I helped wrap the present from Madam and Pop. It is an old black metal box that has blue and green hydrangea flowers painted on it that came from Antiques on the Hill. Madam says the box was for keeping coal in the olden days but she decided it's tall enough to be a little table at the end of the sofa once we ever get one. I put my present in a party bag. "I love this lanyard a lot," I told Madam. "Next, I'm going to make one that will be for me and it will have a necklace like Ashley's."

Just then Pop and Gumbo got back and Madam said, "We'd better shake a leg. Lily will be here at 5:30."

"We'd better shake all our legs," I said.

Pop tied the balloons to my mom's chair and Madam put the lilies in a vase that is so old she got it for a present at her wedding. Then we all set the table with plates that came from Italy and cloth napkins and I made name cards and when we were done Madam said, "Gorgeous!" which was the absolute truth.

It was also in the very nick of time because right then my mom came in the front door and I hollered, "Surprise!"

My mom said, "Oh my goodness! Balloons! And lilies!"

"And those bones you like," I said.

"Then everything is perfect," she said and she

gave me a hug and then Madam and Pop got hugged too.

After dinner came presents. Aunt Marguerite sent a photo that she took of a man riding on a bike. The M.O.T.H.s sent a funny card and the one named Rhonda wrote on it, "29 Forever!" whatever that means. My dad's card had a cake on the front and inside he wrote, "I hope your birthday is a happy one! Bob."

I didn't think this was the best but my mom read it and said, "That's nice." So I think that could be good.

Uncle Mike and Aunt Max mailed her a clock that looks like a cat and has rolling eyes. Aunt Pansy sent chocolate that is divine and deluxe. My mom loved the hydrangea box. But her best present was the key chain from me.

July 14 Countdown: 38 Days

Today, when we were taking Gumbo to the dog beauty shop, I was in charge of the leash and at Stanton Park, I shouted, "Go, dog!" Then Gumbo started running so fast I could almost not hold on and was practically tipping over and I had to yell, "Stop!" a lot before he did.

"What made you tell Gumbo to 'Go, dog'?" my mom said.

"It's my new palindrome," I said. "I wanted to try it out."

"I'm just glad 'Go, snakes!' isn't a palindrome," Pop said. "We'd have a snake stampede every time we went to the zoo."

On the walk back Pop said everybody had to tell one interesting thing that happened this week. My mom said, "Well, my boss told me that nobody had ever drawn a map of Tunisia that looked better than mine."

To show I was proud I called out, "Yippee-yi-yo, cowgirl!"

Madam said, "That's terrific, Lily!"

Pop said, "You're a pro!" which is short for PROfessional.

Then he said, "I'm writing a story about dill pickles so this morning I got 10 jars of them in the mail."

"Next time," I said, "write about gum."

Then Madam said, "Remember when I said it seemed like everyone who wrote to 'Dear Lucy Rose' had a picky eater?"

We did remember.

"Well, now I'm getting a lot of letters from mothers who have little boys who won't behave," Madam said.

"I have a problem with a girl who won't behave," I said.

"You do?" Pop asked me.

I told about Ashley and her mean remarks.

"Maybe she's shy," my mom said.

"Nope," I said. "She also makes snarky looks at people and by people I mean me and Jonique and Melonhead."

"That's crummy," my mom said. "I wonder what is the best way to handle a problem like that."

My mom always says she's wondering when she's really trying to make me think up the answer.

"I know how," Pop said.

"You do?" I said.

"All we need are some clothespins and some very sticky flypaper," he said.

That joke had me laughing my face off.

"You know," Madam said, "I find that often the kids that are the hardest to like are the ones that most need a friend."

"Madam," I said. "I'm not the girl for that job."

Today at Bingo a new lady named Mrs. Fern Edwards won a bottle of TOILET WATER! I felt extremely disgusted when I heard that and I told Ms. Bazoo, "That is the worst prize I ever heard of, especially for a new person."

"It's perfume. It doesn't actually come from the toilet," Ms. Bazoo explained to me.

Here's what I think: The people who invented toilet water will go broke because no one will buy perfume with such a terrible name.

I e-mailed my dad this news and he wrote right back and said, "A lot goes on at the Capitol Hill Home, doesn't it?"

"You are not kidding," I said. "At refreshments Ms. Bazoo recommends people take 2 cookies but today Mrs. Hennessy took 9. I was flabbergasted. Do you ever get flabbergasted?"

"All the time," he wrote.

"You know what flabbergasted means? It means shocked and surprised until you're stunned," I said.

"I know. I am flabbergasted by your vocabulary," he said.

I wrote back: "Guess how I am standing? Akimbo."

Late at night, when I was supposed to be asleep, I figured out a better way to save the apricots.

July 16

I rode my scooter over to Parks & Rec first thing and found Trip and told him, "I am having a serious problem."

"With Ashley?" he asked me.

I was surprised he knew she was a problem. "With squirrels," I said and I told him my plan.

"Nobody ever wants to make this color key chain," Trip said and gave me two whole rolls of gray Gimp.

I put the Gimp spools on my handlebars and zoomed to the McBees' and pressed hard on their doorbell which I love to do because they have the kind that plays the music of "You Make Me Feel Like a Natural Woman" which is the best song of Mrs. McBee's life. I always sing along real loud so they know it's me. Mrs. McBee called out, "Come in, Lucy Rose. Jonique can't go anywhere until I finish braiding her hair."

I knew from experiences that braiding would take quite a little while because Jonique is one for wiggling and that slows the job down. So I went in and sat and told about my new plan.

When Jonique's hair was finally all the way braided she got her scooter and we scooted like mad to Melonhead's and the second I told him, "We're going on the roof," he was ready.

When we got to my grandparents', Pop was in his office so we all yelled "Hi" at him and he called back "Hi" to us. Then he asked Melonhead, "How's the mustache coming along?"

"It's coming, I think," Melonhead said.

We ran upstairs and out the bathroom window and all 3 stood on the breezeway roof, which always gives me the feeling of being thrilled. "We are pretty far from earth," I said.

"Too bad it has railings," Melonhead said.

He is one who likes danger.

"Melonhead, your job is to pull down a tall branch so I can tie Gimp to it," I said, partly to get his mind off the railings.

By the time Madam came home we had that tree covered with zigzagging Gimp. "This will keep those pesky squirrels away," I said and I could tell she was feeling relief.

July 17

This morning Jonique and Melonhead and I raced to Madam and Pop's so we could see our invention working. And here's the thing of it: Instead of no squirrels there were MORE squirrels. Tons more. More than we could count. They were climbing and swinging like they were on trapezes and jumping from Gimp to Gimp grabbing apricots and flinging them on the ground and when you looked at them you could tell it was on purpose.

"I cannot believe my eyes," Melonhead said.

"Believe them. We're having a squirrel emergency," I said.

"We're in the middle of a squirrel circus," Jonique said.

"I think people would pay a lot to see a squirrel circus!" Melonhead said and he started dancing around the yard.

"Kids could pay a quarter!" I said.

"If we got 4 kids we'd have $1 and if we had 20 kids we'd have $5!" Jonique shouted.

Jonique can do multiples that quick on account of she's a lover of math.

"Grown-ups can pay $1," I said. "Pop, call all your friends."

"We'll be made of money," Melonhead said.

Then Madam came through the gate. She was

not feeling thrilled. "I admire a moneymaking scheme as much as the next grandmother," she said. "But the idea is to save the fruit!"

Pop gave Madam a shoulder rub so she wouldn't have stress. Then he said in his nicest voice, "Are you absolutely sure you don't want to go into the squirrel circus business?"

She was. We had to spend a lot of time pulling down that Gimp and picking up green one-bite apricots.

July 18

Even though I'm feeling sick of Gimp, I went to Parks & Rec and started a lanyard key chain that is for me. I picked hot pink and lime green which made Trip say, "Outstanding."

Melonhead came with me, which was too bad because every time Ashley saw him, she put the ends of her braids on her lip so it would look like she had a mustache. "Ignore her," I told Melonhead. "She has no maturity at all."

July 19 Countdown: 33 Days

When I got home there was a postcard on my pillow. On the front was a man carrying a heart in a wheelbarrow and it said, "This is for you." On the back was a note that said: "Greetings from Camp Timberline. Guess who is in Cabin 4? Your pals Annie and Franny Rhineburger. They said to tell you 'Hi' and that they got Ms. Simon for their teacher. Their big sister told them Ms. Simon is a walking nightmare. Now they want to skip 4th grade. See you soon, my little baboon. oxo, Dad. P.S. Pack a bathing suit."

I wrote him a postcard back and said: "Tell those Rhineburgers that I miss them and I haven't met any twins at all in Washington." Then I drew him a picture of me wearing my party skirt and a sweatshirt with my bathing suit top over it with my softball bat in my hand. Then I wrote: "Wherever this adventure is, I am going to look ridiculous."

July 20

My mom and I cooked out. We made burgers and corn on the cob on the grill. Then we sat on the back steps and looked at the fireflies.

Then I said the very thing that I never planned on asking, "Are we getting divorced?"

"We've had a year to see how we feel and Daddy and I think getting divorced is the right thing to do," she answered.

"Nobody asked me," I told her. "And I feel like it is the exact wrong thing to do."

"You're the main reason we tried to work it out," she said.

"Can't we just stay separated instead?" I said.

"I'm sorry but it doesn't work that way," my mom said.

"Ask me how I'm feeling," I said.

"How are you feeling, Lucy Rose?" she said.

"Mad at you, that's how," I told her.

She put her arms around me but I was not in the

mood for that. "Plus I'm extremely crestfallen," I said.

I e-mailed my dad and said, "I say NO DIVORCE."

"I'm sorry," was his message back.

I told him, "Then don't do it."

"I hope you know how much Mom and I love you," he said.

"I do know," I told him. "You should love each other, too."

He wrote back: "Let's talk about it when I come out for the big adventure."

Here's what I did with that idea: I turned off the computer.

I went to Parks & Rec with only Melonhead because Jonique went to work downtown at the government with her dad. She gets to go one time every year to be his assistant and staple papers. And Mr. McBee takes her to a restaurant for lunch. I told Melonhead, "I wish I could go to work with my dad even though it would actually be going to school but at least it would be junior high which would probably be extremely fascinating."

"I've been to my dad's work and it's boring," Melonhead said. "Instead of me going to his work, I wish he would stay home sometimes."

Mr. Melon is a traveler because the congressman he works for has to go a lot of places and Mr. Melon has to go with him even if it's Halloween.

When I got home my mom said, "How are you feeling?"

"P-U," I said.

"I'm sad about that," she said.

"I will tell you one thing: When I am grown up I am never, ever going to get a divorce," I said.

"I hope with all my heart you don't," my mom said. "Divorce is hard on everybody."

We had breakfast for dinner, which is one thing I love to do, and Jonique came over in time to eat a pancake. "I made this for you," she said and gave me a piece of paper. "It's my hand. I put it on the copy machine and pushed Start."

"It is a treasure," I told her.

We took it to my room and taped it to the wall.

Later I gave my mom a hug. But it wasn't the biggest.

July 23

Tonight Madam and Pop came over with 2 chairs that don't get enough use at their house so now they will get lots of it in our living room. They are yellow with skinny dark yellow stripes that are perfect with Banana Frappe, according to my mom.

July 24

The squirrels are making me feel like I am going to get insanity. Every day there are more squirrels in the tree and more apricots on the ground. I think there will be none left for jam.

Plus I had to take out 2 inches of my lanyard because I just noticed I missed a loop. "You have to choose between being quick or being perfect," Trip said.

"I pick perfect on account of I am going to wear this lanyard for my whole life," I told him.

The one good thing is that Jonique is sleeping over with me at Madam and Pop's.

July 25

This morning Jonique and I ate our cereal on the upstairs porch and after every bite I hollered out, "Scram, squirrels."

And Jonique shouted, "Vamoose."

They didn't. When we banged our spoons on the railing they did not even care. Then it started pouring down rain and they did and I knew what to do.

When the sun came out, the squirrels came back but Jonique and I got both hoses and sprayed the tree like it was raining and they skittered away. "We have made a miracle!" I said. "Let's call Melonhead for extra help."

He came right over and we all 3 took turns spraying and our plan kept on working, only after a lot of hours our arms felt aching and our fingers were pruney and that's when we noticed the bark pieces that Pop puts around the tree were looking floaty. "I think we made our own irrigation," Melonhead said.

Then Jonique said, "Yikes! The bottom of the basement steps looks like a little square lake."

When I went down the water came up past the bump of my anklebone. "Oh, this really is not the best," I said.

"Now you can tell Ashley that you have a swimming pool," Melonhead said and started up with his hooty laugh.

"I just I hope we have privacy," I said. "Because this is not the time for any grown-ups to come outside."

Melonhead got beach towels from the mudroom and we started mopping up but those towels didn't

soak up much water at all before they got wet in the extreme and were so heavy that we could hardly pick them up and Jonique's flip-flops were floating and the bottom part of the basement door was underneath water. "Do you think it's getting inside?" Jonique asked me.

"I surely hope not," I told her. "But I'll check."

"Don't open that door!" Melonhead screamed.

Too late. I already had and the thing about water is that it moves fast.

"At least there's no water outside now," Jonique said.

"But some is still coming down the steps," I said.

"We've got to build a dam!" Melonhead said.

We were dragging firewood logs down from the porch when Madam and Pop and my mom all came out the back door.

My mom looked at the yard and said, "What happened?"

"Water keeps squirrels away," I said, pointing at the hoses which I am sorry to say we had not remembered to turn off.

"Excellently," Melonhead said.

"Very excellently," Jonique said.

And then I took a big gasp of air because I knew we were going to get a serious talk.

Pop looked at me and at Melonhead and at Jonique and then back at me and then at the bottom of the steps and I felt terrible. Then he said, "I CANNOT believe you did this. I hardly know what to say."

"I do," my mom said and I could tell from her forehead wrinkles that what she had to say was not going to be pleasing to hear.

But Pop kept talking. "I say this is fantastic! A first-rate idea! Congratulations to you all on your squirrel removing invention. I wish I had thought of it myself."

"I'm sorry about the flooded basement," I said.

"Flood shmud," Pop said. "That is the sort of minor setback that happens to all great inventors."

"They happen to me all the time," Melonhead said.

Madam looked at Pop with her Madam eyes and then she looked at the steps and the water trickle going down them and she said, "Well, if water keeps squirrels away I guess we don't have to worry about the squirrels going into the basement."

"Exactly," Pop said. "Nobody wants squirrels in the basement. That would be unsanitary."

"You are an optimist," I told Madam. That word of the day means a person who thinks things are better instead of worse.

That made Madam laugh. "I must be," she said.

The rest of the day was yuck because we had to mop the basement and sweep water out of the yard and you wouldn't believe how simply beat tired that makes you feel. Also famished. And by the time we finished cleaning, those squirrels were right back in that tree, flinging apricots at us.

"Madam," I said. "I give up. I can't save these apricots."

"I think that might be for the best," she said.

July 26

When we got to Parks & Rec, Melonhead was already there doing woodworking. Jonique and I don't know what he is making because it's a secret but I will tell you one thing: It's not what anybody would call good-looking. It is made of a long board that he is hammering nails through so the points stick up which I told him is a danger. I think he's making it for his parents and I feel sorry about that because if he brings it home they will have to make a display of it just to be polite.

I am in love with my key chain. My box stitch is smooth with no lumps plus I'm wild about the smell of it which is like plastic. Trip showed me how to make my neck loop so it looks like diamonds, the shape, not the jewel. When I ever get finished I'm going to put a key on it and wear it every day and I hope people ask me who made it so I can tell them, "Me."

The good thing about Melonhead's woodworking is that he is away from Ashley, which I am glad of because she cannot stop talking about that mustache that he doesn't have.

July 27

I e-mailed Glamma and I told her, "Here's what I am the queen of: Bingo."

I love being the caller. For one thing everybody listens to you and for another, I am crazy about the microphone. Today after we did 8 games, Ms. Bazoo gave out all the prizes. Mrs. Zuckerman got red slippers made of yarn and Mrs. Hennessy won breath mints and Mrs. Edwards won a little radio which I thought was a good way to make up for the toilet water from before. Then I told Ms. Bazoo what I was going out of my head wanting to do and she let me. Jonique went to the front and said, "Ladies and gentlemen, I am presenting Lucy Rose Reilly."

"Thank you," I said and I made a beautiful curtsy.

Then I stood up on a chair and sang in the microphone "I Love You a Bushel and a Peck and a Hug Around the Neck" from *Guys and Dolls*. I got a lot of clapping, especially from Mrs.

Hennessy who wanted me to sing it all over again so I did.

I told my mom and Pop and Madam about it at dinner. "I was a spectacle," I said.

"I have no doubt about that," Pop said.

Tonight was one of my greatest nights ever. Pop took me to Arena Stage to see his friend named Antonio Rizzoli who is an actor in the musical called *Cats*, which is not the easiest play to understand. Also the songs are not the snappiest but I did love "Memories." I double loved the look of the stage because they had a sardine can that is bigger than the front door of our house which is odd because the actors are supposed to be cats and in real life cats are bigger than sardine cans.

When *Cats* was over, Pop took me to the backstage dressing rooms and Mr. Rizzoli was there still looking like a cat and looking at himself in a mirror that had lights all around it which is how he saw us before we even said hello.

"Come in! Come in!" he said and he waved his arms so we would know he was feeling excited to see us. Then he said, "Lucy Rose, would you like a Coca-Cola?"

"Would I ever," I said.

I was glad I was with Pop because my mom is the type who says "too much caffeine" and Pop is not that type at all. I got to drink it out of the bottle which is the best because it makes my mouth sting but in a good way.

"Have you ever worn stage makeup?" Mr. Rizzoli asked.

"No," I said. "I would love that like anything."

I got to sit in his chair and get cat makeup put on my face. Plus fake eyelashes. Then he said, "How many whiskers?"

"The same as you, 5 on each side," I said.

Then I had to stay extremely still while he dipped a long whisker in a bottle and put the wet end right on my cheek.

"Are you putting glue on my face?" I asked him.

"It's called spirit gum and it's just for actors," he said.

"Just how long will this gum last?" I asked.

"A few days," he said.

"Holy moly," I said.

"Or I can give you gum remover and you can take it off whenever you want," he told me.

"Excellent-O," I said very still-like so he could keep gluing.

When he finished I was hilarious like you couldn't believe and even though my face itched, I loved looking at myself.

When we were leaving Mr. Rizzoli made a bow at me and said, "Come anytime."

"Don't you worry," I said. "We will."

It was 11 o'clock PM at night so instead of going home Pop drove us to my mom's TV station so we could pick her up from the late shift and the guard called her on the telephone and said, "Ms. Reilly, you have a guest in the lobby."

When she saw me she almost fell over from being stunned.

Now I'm home and in my bed, still wearing my cat face, writing in this book. My mom is asleep but I am not on account of the caffeine.

July 29

The apricots aren't too green anymore, but they also aren't orange. Madam says they'll be ready to pick pretty soon. If there are any left.

July 30

I say my dad is smarter than the president is because this is what he e-mailed to me: "Dear Lucy Rose, Do you remember what kind of car I have?"

I e-mailed back, "A Toyota."

"Nice palindrome," he wrote.

Can you believe it?

July 31

Jonique invited me to dinner which was deluxe. We had butter beans and meat loaf and biscuits plus cheesy rice and red Jell-O. But first we all held hands and Mr. McBee said the blessing. Then he said, "How was your day?"

Jonique said: "Very fine. I got to go to the dentist and she gave me a green toothbrush. For free."

"And how about you, Lucy Rose?" he asked.

"It was a superior day," I said. "That means really good."

"It is also a lake," Mr. McBee said. "Lake Superior."

I'd like to see what's so good about that lake one day.

"This was the day I almost finished my key chain," I told him.

AUGUST

August 1

Melonhead was waiting for us at Parks & Rec. "Follow me to woodworking," he said.

There was his project looking just like it did before only with more nails. "Help me carry it to Madam and Pop's," he said.

"I thought it was for your mom and dad," I said.

"They don't need it," he said.

I almost said, "Madam and Pop don't need it either," but I didn't on account of I have maturity.

When we got there Melonhead rang the bell even though the door was open and shouted: "Present delivery for Madam and Pop."

Pop looked at it and said, "It's a work of art."

Then he called for Madam to come see it and she inspected it and said, "Adam, you are a thoughtful boy."

"I think it will look grand in the morning room," Pop said.

"It will look perfect there," Madam agreed.

Jonique gave me a look and I gave her one back. We both thought that idea was P-U.

But Melonhead said, "It's for the backyard."

"Even better," Pop said.

I was one person agreeing with that.

Melonhead put it right in the middle of the patio with all the nails sticking up which, I have to say, looked terrible. Then he said, "Wait here. I'm coming right back."

Pop cut up a baby watermelon and we all sat in the backyard eating it and looking at Melonhead's art. "The important thing is that he has a giving heart," Madam said.

"I can't wait to see what he's going to give us next," Pop said. "It's hard to improve upon a life-threatening sculpture."

Melonhead came back carrying a paper bag and said, "Madam and Pop, go inside. Lucy Rose and Jonique, you stay here."

When they were gone he said, "Take a look at this."

"It looks like the dried-up corn that Mrs. McBee

hangs on the front door when it's Thanksgiving," I had to say.

Melonhead gave us each a corn and told us to stick it on a nail. We had to keep doing it until we had 22 corns sticking straight up in the air which made his art look even uglier, if you ask me. Then he said, "Now, get Madam and Pop."

When we came back we couldn't believe our eyeballs. Squirrels had surrounded Melonhead's invention. "They're eating the corn!" Jonique said.

"It's like they are sitting at a tiny picnic table," I said.

"Amazing!" Madam said.

"Brilliant!" Pop said.

Then I said, "Melonhead, you are the smartest boy I know."

I never thought he would be the one to save the apricots.

August 2

I am wearing my new key chain which is so gorgeous I think it could be for sale at the Mazza

Gallerie for about $11 or more. When I finally finished it this afternoon, Jonique told me, "That is a superior key chain, Lucy Rose."

Trip said, "All right, Lucy Rose!" and gave me a high 5.

Melonhead said, "Awesome!"

And a teenager I don't even know told me, "Way to go!"

Then Ashley looked at it and petted it and made a little smile and said, "Oh well, I guess that's the best you can do."

"I feel steaming at her," I told Madam when I got home.

"She must be an unhappy person to act that way," Madam said.

I say I am an unhappy person because she acts that way.

August 3

When my mom came to pick me up at my grandparents' I was waiting on the front porch wearing my new key chain and she hugged me and said, "You've got a real talent for Gimp."

"Plus a flair," I said.

"Definitely a flair," she said. "Let's take a picture of you wearing your key chain and we can e-mail it to Dad."

So we did. And my dad called it beauteous.

August 4

For 3 days there has not been 1 single apricot on the ground because the only thing the squirrels care about now is corn. Madam bought a pile of dried-up corn cores from Mrs. Calamaris and every day we take off the used-up ones and put on new old corn.

August 5

Today my mom was the one with a plan. I knew it the second I went outside because there was a huge yellow square in our very little yard and all around it were paper plates with squoogles of paint that were the colors of all the paint cards we liked. "What on earth is this?" I said.

"Canvas," my mom said. "I decided that what the living room needs is a painting and that we are just the artists to paint it."

"Excellent-O," I said. "I vote for abstract because I saw some on our field trip to the Hirshhorn Museum and it is wild."

"Perfect. You make the first stroke," my mom said.

I made a giant Raspberry swoop and then I put on some Conch Shell and my mom painted Celery and Sage zigzags. I mixed Sunset and Lemon Meringue into the jazziest orange ever and painted things that look kind of like hearts. My mom put in some Ivory which didn't look dull next to Caribbean. Then we stopped because it was a masterpiece. "Every time I see it, I will think of this happy day," my mom said and then we had a hug.

"Me too," I said. "Happy Day should be its name."

What was unhappy was that while my mom went inside to answer the phone, guess who walked right in front of our house? Ashley, that's who. She stopped and said, "What's that?"

"My mom and I painted it for our living room," I told her. "It's abstract."

"It looks like throw-up," she said and walked away fast.

"It does not!" I hollered but she didn't turn around.

When my mom came out I told her about that throw-up remark and she said, "Poor girl, she must be jealous."

"Whatever she is, it's not jealous," I said.

Now Happy Day is hanging on the biggest wall in the living room. And it does not look anything like throw-up.

August 6 Countdown: 15 Days

At Bingo I was the spinner and Jonique was the caller. Her voice was a little quiet because she wasn't too near the microphone which made Mrs. Hennessy holler out, "I can't HEAR you."

Every time Jonique called out a B, Mrs. Hennessy said, "B what?"

Finally Mrs. Zuckerman said, "Behave."

Mrs. Hennessy has been extra pippish. She

keeps calling Jonique Monique and calling me Red. She says it's because of my hair but I think maybe she can't remember Lucy Rose. Today when Ms. Bazoo gave her a letter that came from her son that's a nurse who lives in New Mexico, she put it down and lost it and Jonique and I had to look absolutely everywhere until we found it with her keys and her little pack of Kleenex on the magazine table. When we gave it back to her she showed us a picture of the son and the son's wife. I told her, "Your son is handsome looking."

"He looks like my father when he was young," she said.

So I guess she is remembering the important things.

August 6 Late at night

I CANNOT wait for my dad and our adventure. But I CAN wait FOREVER to have that divorce talk.

Guess what we did? Got a sofa, that's what. We shopped our legs off. It was my mom's job to choose the style and Madam's job to tell what was good and what was bad about every couch. My job was to lie down and say if it was comfortable. The first one my mom liked had yellow and pink lines but bad springs, according to Madam.

At the next store Madam said, "This one's so sturdy that Lucy Rose will be in college before you need a new one."

"But it's plaid," my mom said.

She is not one for plaid which makes me say thank goodness because neither am I.

Nobody liked the sofas in the store that came after that.

Finally, when we were exhausted to pieces plus starving practically to death we went to a store that had my mom's perfect sofa right in the window. "Look! Periwinkle blue with white piping!" my mom said. Piping is what's on the edges and now it's my word of the day.

Madam examined it and said, "Good springs. Well made."

Since I was the tester, the man let me climb right in the window and lie down on the sofa. "It's like a cloud," I said.

"It's a floor model," the man said. "I'll give you a deal."

We took that deal and my mom wrote a check and workers tied the sofa to the roof of Madam's station wagon and we drove it home and now that sofa is in our living room looking like it's gorgeous.

The rule is family can't eat on it. Only company.

August 8

Pop called and said: "Gather the troops and come on over."

I put on my Go Blue T-shirt with cutoff shorts and my boots and my key chain and my green plastic visor that I got last year at Sam Alswang's birthday party for extra added protection. Melonhead and Jonique got to Madam and Pop's in a flash.

Madam gave us baskets that are called bushel and all 3 of us, plus Pop, climbed out the bathroom window and stood on top of the breezeway and Pop said, "The sun is shining and the apricots are ripe and all's right with the world."

And you know what? All was right because even though the squirrels had ruined lots of apricots, there were still about a thousand left. "That is because of your great invention," I told Melonhead which was a complimenting thing for me to say, especially since he is one for saying it himself.

Then Pop said, "Let the picking begin! But remember apricots are fragile creatures. Don't fling them into the basket because they'll turn to mush."

Picking was easy because even when they are all the way grown, apricots are a puny fruit. Jonique and Pop were the fastest. I was the next fastest. Melonhead was slow because he kept eating his apricots. I was roasting so I had to pat my face all over with my bandana for refreshment.

"Who's hungry?" Pop said after we loaded 1 basket.

"I'm famishing," Melonhead said and then he told Pop, "That means starving to death."

"Pop was the first one to know that word," I said because Melonhead was acting like he invented it.

"I'm thirsty and hungry," Jonique said.

"Same for me," I said.

"I'll see what I can scare up for lunch," Pop said which made Jonique look nervous.

I think he saw because he said, "How do you feel about a cabbage sandwich, Jonique?"

She shook her head no but Melonhead said, "I'll have one." And he would too because he will eat anything.

Pop gave us a warning that we should not fool around and climbed through the window, which shut itself a minute later. And was extremely stuck.

"Pop will be back soon," Melonhead said.

"Not so soon. He is a slow kind of cook," I said.

"I have to go to the bathroom," Jonique whispered to me.

"I have sympathy for that because I know how it is when there is no bathroom to go to," I said. "Let's knock on the window."

Pop didn't hear us. So then I started singing "I'm Always True to You, Darlin'" from *Kiss Me Kate* so Mrs. Napper would come and tell us to stop and we could ask her to get Pop. Only she didn't and after a while I figured out that she was not home. I was feeling too much heat and Melonhead was eating too many apricots and Jonique had too much anxiety. Then I spied somebody walking down Fifth Street and I hollered, "Hey, girl!"

She looked up and it's lucky I wasn't near the edge or I could have fallen off from shock on account of the girl was Ashley. "What are YOU doing up there?" she yelled at us.

"Picking apricots," I said.

"But we got locked out," Melonhead explained to her.

"Now we're trapped on the roof," Jonique said.

"Could you PLEASE knock on the front door

and ask my grandfather to come open the window?" I shouted to her.

Ashley looked at all 3 of us and said, "No."

"Please?" Melonhead shouted.

"I'm desperate to go to the bathroom," Jonique said.

"Too bad. So sad," Ashley said and started walking away.

That made me so steaming that before my head even knew what my arm was doing I threw an apricot straight at her and it hit her right on her butt and smooshed right into mush.

"I'm sorry! I didn't mean to hit your butt. I actually didn't mean to hit you at all," I yelled down to her.

"You're in BIG trouble, Lucy Rose," she screamed back.

Then she turned and went the other way and we could tell how mad she was because all the way up on the roof we could hear her stompy footsteps. "I am in for it now," I said.

"True but I think you saved the day for me," Jonique said.

Which I did because Pop came up in 2 seconds

and opened the window and let us in and said, "Lucy Rose, there is a girl downstairs."

"I know," I said.

"Madam asked her to sit but she said she can't because she has mashed apricot on the seat of her shorts," he said.

When I got downstairs Ashley was standing in the morning room looking furious in the extreme and Gumbo was dancing around her which he does when he is trying to be nice but it just made her more steaming. Then Madam said, "Lucy Rose, I think you have something to say to Ashley."

Even though I had already said it, I said it again. "I'm sorry I hit you in the bottom with the apricot I didn't even know it would explode like that."

I said bottom because Madam does not approve of saying butt.

"You should be sorry, Lucy Rose. Very sorry," Ashley said.

"I am very sorry. I am not one for hitting people with apricots," I told her and to show I was TRULY

SORRY I asked her, "Would you like to eat lunch with us?"

"I would not," she said. "Not at all."

Then she said goodbye to Madam but not me and left and Pop got busy making us BLTs with turkey bacon while Madam gave me a big talk. "Did you learn a lesson?" Madam asked me.

"Yes," I said. "But she was going to leave us on the roof and she didn't care about Jonique having to go to the bathroom and I was practically fainting from heat."

"No matter how angry you get you can't throw anything at a person," Madam said. "Even small things like apricots."

"I know that," I said.

"I know you do," Madam said.

"She has been mean to us the whole summer long," I said.

Madam just nodded.

"I know you think she's unhappy and that's why she acts totally P-U," I said. "But you're wrong because she has an aunt with a pool and an excellent key chain and a perfect life."

"We never know about other people's lives," Madam said.

"Okay," Pop called out from the kitchen. "The apricot incident is behind us and the BLTs are in front of us and at least Lucy Rose did figure out a way to get back inside."

Then he said he thought we had done enough apricot picking for one day.

August 9

Madam had to cook the apricots into jam but she let us keep the ones without any bruises. We made them look stylish in a basket and took them to Bingo day. You would not believe how much the retired loved those apricots.

Mrs. Hennessy said, "These are as fresh as rain."

Mrs. Zuckerman said, "They remind me of when I was a little girl." I don't know why.

Mr. Woods said, "Young ladies, you have made my day."

And nobody could believe that we climbed on the roof to get them and that our parents let us.

Now that Jonique has the knack, she does all the Bingo calling which is fair because I do all the singing. Today my song was "A Hundred and One Pounds of Fun That's My Little Honeybun," from *South Pacific*. Afterward I said, "My mom weighs 110 or more pounds."

And the people went wild with clapping.

It was one of the best afternoons we have had at the Capitol Hill Home until refreshments when Mrs. Hennessy made everyone get up because she lost her apricots. When Mr. Woods found them under her chair, she told him, "Thank you, Emanuel. I just can't keep track of my things anymore."

August 11

Madam thinks Gumbo is the smartest dog in America. I do not think so. Today he went under the apricot tree and rolled around until his whole back was covered with dirt. Pop and my mom and I had to give him a bath in the bathtub, which is absolutely a 3-person job. Seeing all that dirt made Pop ask me, "How is Jonique's camping plan coming along?"

"She gave up," I told him. "Her parents are still totally against camping and we tried Madam's idea of finding someone else to take us but Mom has overtime and Madam says your backs are too old, so we are out of ideas."

"What if you and Jonique and Melonhead camped out in our far backyard?" Pop said.

"By ourselves?" I said.

"Sure," he said.

"That's a terrific idea. If you get scared you can always come inside," my mom said.

"We won't get scared," I told her.

"Of course not," Pop said.

Even though my arms were soaking and covered with soap bubbles, I gave him the most gigantic hug.

Later I told Mr. and Mrs. McBee: "The far backyard is really near. You get there by walking through the garage that used to be a stable for horses in the really olden days. So you don't have one thing to worry over."

"Sounds good to me," said Mrs. McBee.

"Very good," Mr. McBee said.

Jonique and I had to dance around the McBees' living room for quite a little while.

August 12

I went to Parks & Rec just to make an effort with Ashley. "I really am sorry about throwing that apricot at you," I told her.

"Did you get in trouble after I left?" she asked me.

"Yes," I said.

"Good," she said.

I took a gasp of air and made my voice top-volume and said: "Ashley, you are on my last nerve. Jonique and I and Melonhead try to be nice to you but we are giving up because you are the snarkiest girl in America."

"It was mean to throw apricots at me," she said.

"One apricot," I said. "And I said I was sorry. You have been mean all summer long. You act like you don't like us."

"I don't," she said, which even though I don't like her was not a pleasing thing to hear.

"Are you acting like this because you're unhappy?" I asked her. "Because if it is, I know how you feel."

"You certainly do not know how I feel," she said. "You and Jonique and Melonhead have probably been friends since preschool and nobody got divorced and made you move to a little house without a pool. And your dad is not living 20 miles away in Potomac, Maryland."

That shocked me so much that I just stood there and stared at her for the longest time. "No," I finally said. "He lives in Ann Arbor, Michigan, which is over 500 miles away."

But Ashley was already stomping off. Then when she was halfway across the playground she turned around and yelled: "On top of everything, you are a nosey snoop, Lucy Rose."

Later I told Pop the whole story. "I understand how she feels but not how she acts," I said. "I'm DONE with that girl."

"Luckily, you only have to see her at Parks & Rec," Pop said. "Think of her as a summertime pest. Like mosquitoes."

"If she was a mosquito I could keep her away with Bug-B-Gone," I said.

"Want to go see if Congress Market has any Ashley-Away spray?" Pop said.

They didn't, of course, because that was a joke. But we did get cherry Popsicles which helped with the cheering up.

August 13

When we got to the Capitol Hill Home Mrs. Hennessy was having a disaster. "I can't find my keys," she said.

"I'll help you look for them," Ms. Bazoo told her.

"Us too," I said.

"They're probably on the sofa," Jonique told her. But they weren't.

"I'll check the magazine table," I said.

They weren't there, either.

Ms. Bazoo pulled the cushion off of a chair but all she found was somebody's lost comb. Mr. Woods looked under all the tables and Mrs. Hennessy just looked sad.

"Don't worry," Ms. Bazoo said. "We always find them."

"I know. It's just that when I was young, I remembered everything. I would never forget my purse or lose my keys. I guess I will have to pin them to my dress," Mrs. Hennessy said.

"No you won't," I told her.

Then I took my key chain necklace off and put the loop around her neck.

Right then Mrs. Zuckerman came up and patted Mrs. Hennessy on her arm and said, "Here they are, Flora. You left them on the windowsill."

I unhooked my key and hooked Mrs. Hennessy's keys on the clip. "Now they'll never be lost," I told her.

"Thank you, Red," Mrs. Hennessy said. "This must have taken a long time to make."

"Not that long," I said. "I can always make another one."

"You are a kind girl," she said and she gave me a hug.

Here is the odd thing: Even though I love that key chain, I felt good that I gave it away.

August 14 Countdown: 7 Days

Guess what today is? The day the lady with the baby comes back to work and my mom stops working overtime! To celebrate, Madam and Pop came over to eat salmon which is a fish that my mom says is extremely essential for your body. Essential is my word of the day. It means you've got to have it so I do even though I'd rather not. I made a toast with my sparkling cider: "Here's to the living room and the paint and the sofa and the hydrangea table and the rug and the coffee table and the chairs and the bookshelves and the painting by us!"

"Here's to our home, sweet home," my mom said.

August 15

Pop checked the Weather Channel and said, "It's going to be a perfect night for camping."

Melonhead put himself in charge of supplies. "We have Junior Mints from Mrs. McBee, trail mix and bottles of water from Madam, and the saltine crackers from me," he said.

"Plus 3 flashlights and 3 sleeping bags," I said.

Finally it got to be night but all the parents stood around talking for a huge long time until I had to whisper to Pop, "I think it's time for them to go home."

He got them going but first everybody had to come look at the far backyard. Madam gave us a cooler for our food and said, "Come inside if you get cold."

Mrs. Melon said, "I'm only a phone call away."

Mrs. McBee told Jonique, "Better you than me, Sweetpea."

After they left the first thing we did was brush our teeth and spit on the grass. Then we got in our sleeping bags and hopped across the yard and climbed on the hammock and looked at the backs of houses. We saw the Golds, who are adults but let me call them Amy and Ed which I appreciate. "Amy is holding their dog, Nutmeg, like he is an absolute infant," I said.

Mrs. Pulansky was carrying her real infant

around her upstairs porch trying to get him to sleep which is hard because he is not a sleeping kind of baby. She was singing "Camptown Ladies" and when it got to the Doodah part we sang with her but not too loud because we didn't want to make the crying worse. She looked over and waved at us really nice.

Then Jonique said, "Look at the Johnsons' house!"

Mr. Johnson was standing by the window brushing his little amount of hair, wearing his red polka-dotty boxer underpants which was so hilarious that our laughing made the hammock shake. Then Melonhead shined his flashlight on Mr. Johnson's window which made us terrified out of our minds because what if Mr. Johnson caught us? We turned off our lights double fast and rolled out of the hammock and lay real quiet not breathing on the ground for ages and when it was safe we rolled over to the grape arbor with our bodies still in our sleeping bags.

By then we needed a snack. Jonique put Junior Mints on her eyes and then she turned the flashlight on her face and stuck out her tongue and that made Melonhead squish Junior Mints on his teeth so it looked like some had fallen out and I made Junior Mint earrings which weren't really funny at all but Jonique laughed anyway because she's my true friend. Then Melonhead told a story about a hitchhiking ghost. After a while all the lights in all the houses went out and we were completely in the dark.

Melonhead was the first one to sleep and then Jonique and I just lay in the dark. "I am a happy camper," she said.

Even in the dark I could tell that was true.

Then Jonique was sleeping too. Now I'm writing by flashlight and the cricket sounds are making me feel nervous.

August 16, report on last night

I think I was almost all the way asleep when I heard he-he noises that made my eyes fly open and then came little step noises and I was so scared and wishing I was inside and thinking about Melon-head's story. I didn't want to look but then I did and boy, did I feel relief to see Pop and Madam.

I flashed my flashlight at them and Pop put his finger on his lips in the Shhh way. They were wearing their pajamas and slippers and their odd eyeglasses and Madam was carrying a bag. Pop whispered, "Lucy Rose, come here."

I wiggled right out of my sleeping bag and followed them to the stable and Pop was serious in the extreme. "We are on a secret mission and must operate in the CONE OF SILENCE," he said.

I love the cone. That is our family word for total secret. When he said his plan, I said, "Pop, you are the brilliant one!"

We sneaked back into the far backyard with me carrying Pop's Pocketlite that just makes a tiny dot of light and Pop carrying tiny scissors and Madam holding a bottle of spirit gum that Pop borrowed from Mr. Rizzoli. When we got near the sleeping bags Pop and I got down on our knees. Madam couldn't because she was having a fit of giggling.

I shined the light on the back of Adam Melon's

head and Pop took the tiny scissors and cut off a little of the hair by his neck. Then he said, "Spirit gum," and Madam handed him the bottle and Pop painted gum under Melonhead's nose. Then Melonhead started to roll so Pop had to be quick.

Then Madam and Pop raced back to the house and I tried to sleep and I guess I did because Melonhead woke me up when it was light out and he had to go to the bathroom. I shook Jonique awake and said, "Come on!"

When we got inside Melonhead was dancing around in front of the hall mirror shouting, "I said I'd grow a mustache and I did!"

Pop was in the kitchen doing cross words and he looked up and said, "And it's a nice full one, Adam. Very handsome."

"I can't wait for Parks & Rec to open," Melonhead said.

"We're going with you," I told him.

When we got there, Melonhead walked right by the crafts table and said, "Hey, Ashley."

Ashley looked at him like she had seen the hitchhiking ghost. "You've got a mustache!" she said.

"Of course I do," Melonhead told her.

One of the teenagers said, "It's probably fake."

Ashley got close to the mustache and stared at it hard. "It can't be fake," she said. "It's the same color as his hair."

August 17 Countdown: 4 Days

We were relaxing in the McBees' backyard when Jonique said, "Are you about to bust from excitement waiting for your dad to get here?"

"Yep, I am," I told her.

"It'll be a family reunion," she said.

"You can't have a family reunion with only 2 people," I said.

"Sure you can," Jonique said.

The next thing I knew she told her mom and Mrs. McBee got one of Mr. McBee's newest undershirts, one of Jonique's, and her art supply box and her iron. She had us ironing on letters that said REILLY FAMILY REUNION. "These shirts are the greatest," Jonique said.

I agreed but just for politeness.

August 18 Countdown: 3 Days

Melonhead's mustache has been getting skinnier every day and his lip is looking grayish because spirit gum also works for sticking dirt. By tonight it was almost gone but he didn't seem to care. He told Pop he might grow another one next summer.

August 19 Countdown: 2 Days

We put Jonique's colored pencils and drawing book in her backpack for when she starts vacation Bible school in 2 days. She didn't need clothes because it's not overnight.

Then we packed my plaid suitcase with 1 dress-up skirt plus top, sandals plus sneakers, my purse with $5 from Glamma and $5 more from Pop, my Capitol Hill Arts Workshop sweatshirt, jeans, PJs, T-shirts and shorts, 1 toothbrush plus sunblock because when you have red hair you have to wear that goop every second. Jonique put in the reunion shirts and I didn't take them out because that would be rude in the extreme but I'm not giving it to my dad because I still don't think you can have a family reunion with only half a family.

August 20 Countdown: 1 Day!!

We had my early birthday dinner tonight because if we waited until I got back it would be belated, which means late which is my word of the day. I got to pick dinner and I picked chicken fingers and strawberry shortcake made by Madam. My mom gave me a bracelet that is made of real silver and has a tiny Capitol on it. Jonique gave me Mancala which is one of my best games. Madam and Pop's present was huge and squishy. When I opened it, it unrolled into a long flat pillow covered in fat blue and white striped cloth.

"Madam made it with her sewing machine," Pop said.

"Guess what it's for?" Madam asked me.

"I don't have any idea in this world," I told her.

"Follow us," Pop said and he carried it to the living room.

He put the pillow on the window seat. "Now you have your own special place to hang out," Madam said.

I lay down on that pillow and it felt like I was relaxed.

August 21

I woke up before the alarm and I got dressed and put bagels on a plate so my mom and I could have a bon voyage breakfast in her bed.

"You'll have a great time with your dad," my mom said.

"Do you know where I'm going?" I asked her.

"Yep, but I'm not telling," she said.

At 10 o'clock AM there was honking in front of our house and there was a red car and the driver was my dad, which made me run outside screaming my head off. He was so happy to see me that he picked me up in the air and made me spin around.

Then I said, "This is not A TOYOTA."

"Nope," he said. "It's a rental car. I got it at the

airport because we need wheels to get where we're going."

"For the fancy, sporty, hot, cold adventure," I said.

"Exactly," he said.

My mom waved from the porch and said, "Hi, Bob! Do you want to come in for an English muffin before you leave?"

"Great idea! Dad loves English muffins," I said.

"We should get on the road," my dad said.

"We have time for one puny muffin," I said.

We went inside and I gave him a tour of the new living room. "Madam and Pop helped us paint," I said.

"It's terrific," my dad said.

"It's Banana Frappe," I told him.

My mom fixed a muffin with honey butter which is how he likes it and I was glad she remembered. "You can't eat on the new sofa," I told him because I didn't want him to be company.

Then my mom asked about Glamma and Dad said she was helping out at the Beauty Spot so Shiralee could have a vacation. And when it was time to go I gave my mom the hardest hug of her life. She gave it back and my dad said, "We'll call when we get there and on Lucy Rose's birthday."

We drove until we were far from the city and over the Bay Bridge. We passed cows and farms and irrigation and then we stopped for lunch. I had a cheeseburger and a Sprite. My dad had the same plus onion rings. Then we drove forever to a farm stand for cantaloupe and peaches and double yolk eggs and then it was back in the car for miles more until I was feeling extremely bored of riding when all of a sudden we parked by a totem pole that had giant faces on it and right next to it was a sign that said, WELCOME TO BETHANY BEACH, DELAWARE.

Which is one place I always wanted to go.

August 22

Instead of a hotel we are living in a cottage. It has a kitchen and a living room and 2 bedrooms and a bathroom inside and an extra shower outside. The yard is made of sand and I'm crazy about it. My dad cooked pirate eggs for breakfast plus cantaloupe smiles and then he said, "You're going to need your bathing suit today."

"Yippee-yi-yo, cowgirl!" I said because in my whole life I had never seen an ocean.

When I did I was amazed. The ocean is named the Atlantic but if I was in charge I would take the name of Superior away from the lake and give it to this ocean. It goes out as far as you can see which is actually miles and in the high tide the waves knock you over but in a good way. We stayed all day because even though I was famished I couldn't stand to leave. Here's my list of what we did:

1. Rode the raft.
2. Made a sand castle with a moat and a drawbridge.
3. Saw dolphins jumping.
4. Saw a plane with a streamer sign on back that said EAT MORE CRABS!
5. Took pictures of me.
6. Dug up sand crabs and let them crawl around on our hands.
7. Made wigs out of seaweed.

8. Found a horseshoe-crab shell which is as big as a big plate and has a long pointy horn in front. I am bringing it to Melonhead for a present.
9. Took a long walk.

On the walk my dad asked me, "Do you want to talk about the divorce now?"

I said, "Not yet."

Back at the cottage I had an outside shower and jumped into my shorts and boots and we went to Grotto Pizza and I ate 4 pieces, which is the same as HALF a whole pizza.

I call this day glorious.

August 23

This morning my dad said, "Good morning, sports fans!"

"What do you mean?" I asked him.

"No time to explain. Put this melon in your mouth, your feet in your sneakers, and your body in the car and don't forget your baseball bat," he said.

I had no idea what he was up to until we got to the Batting Cage which is where softballs come flying at you and all you do is try to hit them. I missed a lot. "I'm feeling exasperation," I said.

"Just watch the ball and take your time," he told me.

I took too much time and the ball went right past me but my dad said, "Good try," anyway.

Then when I was about to give up, I hit it! And I kept on hitting it a lot of the time. And my dad was jumping around, cheering for me which is exactly what I would have been doing if it wouldn't make me miss the ball because I will tell you hitting those balls made me feel extremely splendid.

After that we ate hot dogs and tutti-frutti sno-cones and went back to the beach to bounce around in the ocean.

At night we got groceries and cooked chicken and beans in our kitchen. Then we went outside to look for shooting stars and I told him, "I miss living in a house with you."

"I miss living in a house with you, too," he said and gave me a hug.

August 24

My dad woke me up by singing "Happy Birthday."
Then he did a birthday dance that was hilarious
in the extreme. For breakfast I got waffles with 9
birthday candles sticking in them.

Then we went out and I took my $10 to buy
presents for the people at home. "I can't believe all
the great things they sell on this boardwalk," I said.

"Unbelievable is the only word for it," my
dad said.

We decided my mom would love a box that has
teensy shells glued all over it and cost $3.59. I got
Madam a mermaid magnet that has a sparkling tail
for $4.00, which is a ton of money. Pop's present is
a back scratcher shaped like a long, skinny, green
arm with a hand on the end that says BETHANY
BEACH on it. I have $1.22 cents left for Jonique's
present.

For my birthday lunch we got chili dogs and
lemonade and French fries and sat on the boardwalk bench for a picnic. I was telling about Parks &

Rec when all of a sudden a seagull flew down and snatched my dad's fry right out of his hand and flew off. The old lady sitting next to my dad said, "Those birds rankle me."

"That means irritate," my dad told me.

"That's a fine word of the day," I said. Then I told him about Ashley rankling me and he had sympathy for that. "Madam thinks she acts like that because she's unhappy that her parents are getting a divorce," I told him.

"Really?" my dad said.

"Yes, but I don't think so because I am unhappy that my parents are getting a divorce and most of the time I am nice."

For dessert we got a sack of salt-water taffy for us and a box for my dad to take to Glamma. It weighs 1 pound which means I equal 58 boxes of taffy. I thought about getting Swedish fish for Jonique but I decided that wasn't such an exciting present unless I actually got them in Sweden.

We went to the beach for the afternoon and my dad put up the umbrella and I looked out for dolphins while he read his book and the next thing that happened was I fell asleep only I didn't know until I woke up and then I was mad because another thing that rankles me is wasting a day at the ocean. "I'm glad you slept. We've got a big night ahead," my dad said.

Back at the cottage we called my mom and Madam and Pop and they all got on the phone and sang "Happy Birthday" and made kissing noises. Then we called Glamma for another "Happy Birthday." I don't know where we're going but my dad is wearing a shirt that he had to iron. I have on my party clothes and no bandana and no cowgirl boots on account of they are not the thing to wear when you are being fancy, according to Madam.

August 24 but at 11 PM at night

We went to the Magnolia Inn which is so beauteous I wish Mrs. McBee could see it. They have twinkle lights in the trees and when we went inside a man told us, "Good evening."

"We have reservations for Reilly," my dad said.

"Very good, Mr. Reilly. Come this way," the man said.

"I've never had reservations before," I told my dad.

We went right that way to a table that had a white cloth and a candle on it. Here's what I noticed: I was the only kid in the whole Magnolia Inn.

Then a waiter said, "May I take your order?"

My dad told him the food we wanted and then said, "Iced tea for me and a Shirley Temple for the lady, please."

That made me feel mortified. "Shirley Temple is a girl who tap dances, Dad," I said. "Pop and I rented movies of her."

"She was such a great tap dancer they named a drink after her," my dad said.

"That's a news flash to me," I said.

My Shirley Temple came with 2 cherries stabbed on a plastic sword. My dad held his iced tea up in the air and said, "Here's to a happy year for the greatest 9-year-old in the world!"

Then he gave me curled-up paper that was tied

up with string. When I unrolled it, I saw the words "Pals for my Pal" and a list. "It's all the palindromes we have collected this summer and I left space at the bottom for new ones," my dad said.

"This is a great present. I'm going to tape it in the back of my book so I can keep track from now on," I said.

After we ate our salad that had walnuts in it my dad gave me a box and said, "This one is from Glamma."

It was a shirt with a cursive L on it and it's a beaut.

Then the waiter came and my dad gave me a bite of his halibut which he loved but I was not wild for and I gave him one of my raviolis which I was wild for and so was he. We took a long time eating. Afterwards my dad said, "Excuse me," and left the table, which made me wonder if people would think I came to the Magnolia Inn by myself. He came back with a present that had golden wrapping paper and looking at it made my whole stomach feel full from excitement and also ravioli.

"I've been hiding this in the trunk of the car," he said.

At the same second, the waiter came back with 2 plates of chocolate cake and my piece had a candle in it.

"What are you wishing for?" my dad asked me.

"I can't tell or it won't come true," I said and I blew it out.

"Ready to open your present?" Dad said.

"Am I ever!" I told him.

And when I did I jumped up so fast my chair fell over. "These are the most gorgeous cowgirl boots in America," I said. "And I needed them like anything because my toes are right up to the ends in my other pair."

"I thought they'd be running small about now," he said.

Right there in the Magnolia Inn I put on my new, shining red, patent leather with white stars on the front cowgirl boots. And I have to say, I look like a million.

Guess what's different about me since yesterday? More freckles. They come from the sun which is okay because Pop says only the luckiest people get them and he must be right because here's what we did today:

1. Rode rafts in the ocean.
2. Buried my dad in the sand so only his head showed.
3. Went to our cottage and put on jeans and a sweatshirt and my new cowgirl boots.
4. Went to Bucket O' Pasta for dinner and they brought our spaghetti and meatballs in a BEACH PAIL that had a SHOVEL instead of a spoon.
5. Went to Funland.

At Funland we went on the Ferris wheel which is so high you can't believe it and your legs just hang in the air and I was worrying that my new cowgirl boots would fall off and bop somebody on the head but they didn't. We rode on the little kid helicopters and with the teenagers on the Viking ship which swung so high your lungs had to scream. Then we did Teacups which went around and around and when we got off Dad said, "I don't think it's a great idea to experience Bucket O' Pasta and Teacups in the same night."

Then my dad did Ball Toss which is where you throw a Wiffle ball so it lands in a cup but the crummy thing is most of the cups are white and you don't win anything for white. If you get a green cup you get a little stuffed animal. To get a medium one you have to land it in a yellow cup. To win the panda that's as big as me you have to get the ball in the only red cup there is but the man said nobody has been able to do that for the whole summer long.

My dad got 8 balls for $2 and then he got 8 white cups. "Four more balls," my dad told the man.

He got white again. And again. And then he got green and said, "Pick your prize, Lucy Rose."

"The pink octopus," I said. "I mean the blue dolphin. No, the yellow starfish."

By the time I went back to the dolphin I could tell that man was out of patience with me. But just when we were leaving he said, "Mister, you've got one ball left."

"Give it a toss, Lucy Rose," my dad said.

So I did and a red light and a siren went off. Guess why? Because I got red. Which means I got the panda. Which means I have the best present ever for Jonique McBee.

August 26

Since it's the day of our bon voyage we got up early so we could take a last walk on the beach. We were keeping our eyes peeled for good shells when my dad said, "This was the greatest vacation."

"I'm one person who agrees with that," I said.

Then he said, "You are the greatest daughter."

"That's good, because you are the greatest dad," I said. "And I am glad you are the exact way you are."

That is the absolute truth.

When we got back to the cottage I opened up my packed suitcase, put on my Reilly Family Reunion T-shirt, and then I gave my dad his shirt because I figured out that Jonique was right, even though we were just 2 people it was a family reunion.

"I love this shirt," my dad said.

"Me too," I said. And I did.

Now my dad and I and Jonique's giant panda bear are in the rental car driving home. Melonhead's horseshoe crab is riding in the trunk because it smells.

August 26 but at night

After hours of driving we got back to Capitol Hill and my mom ran out to meet us and my dad got my suitcase out of the trunk and then we all went inside and my mom said, "Are you 2 up for lasagna?"

I could see there were 3 plates on the table and my dad said, "I'm always up for your lasagna, Lily."

"Because it's absolutely delightful tasting!" I said.

While we ate I told my mom about the beach

and my mom and my dad told the story of before I was born and how my mom's stomach was so big that when she was standing up and looking down she couldn't see her own shoes and how my dad was so nervous that they got lost driving to the hospital. Then my dad said, "It's time we talked about me and Mom, Lucy Rose."

Which is the very thing I did not want to talk about. "Do we have to get a divorce?" I said.

"Mom and I are getting a divorce, Lucy Rose, but you are not," my dad said. "I won't be her husband and she won't be my wife but you will always be our daughter and we will always love you."

This made me cry harder than ever in my life even counting the time the seesaw crunched my foot and I had to go to the emergency room. "This is not fair to me," I yelled and I put my head down on the table so they could not look at me in the eyes.

"You're right," my dad said.

"But you're doing it anyway!" I shouted. "And I don't get a vote and it's my family too, you know. Did you ever think about that?"

"We are still your family," my mom said.

"When you are an old woman, we will still be your family," my dad told me.

"Do you still love Dad?" I asked Mom.

"We still care about each other but not in the same way," she said.

"Can't you just love each other again?" I asked them.

"No," my dad said.

"We would if we could," my mom said. "It just doesn't work that way."

Which makes no sense to me. "Some divorced people act mean to each other," I said.

"We'll never do that," my dad said.

"Never," my mom said. "That's a promise."

"From both of us," my dad said.

"Are you sorry you got married?" I asked my dad.

"I'm glad we got married because we had you and having you is the very best thing that ever happened to me," he said.

"And to me," my mom said. "The very best."

I got up and went to the living room and lay down on my window seat and cried for the longest time. After a while my parents came in the room. "It really will be okay," my dad said.

"I just want it to be different," I said. "I want us to be like the McBees and have dinner every night and you could help Mom make things and we could all live in one house."

After a while we all 3 took a walk and I walked in the middle holding both of their hands and even though we were all feeling sad, it also felt nice.

August 27

This morning when I got up Madam and Pop and Jonique and Melonhead were knocking on our door and I opened it and everybody hugged me like mad and Jonique hugged her panda and me and while we were hugging my dad came over from the hotel which made Pop say, "This calls for a celebration!"

"Breakfast at Jimmy T's!" I said.

"I'll lead the way!" Melonhead said, pointing ahead with the horseshoe crab which he loves so much he doesn't even think it smells.

On the walk over Jonique told about vacation Bible school which made my mom think about regular school and she said, "I just remembered, I have great news! Do you remember that M.O.T.H. named Rhonda?"

"The 'Forever 29' lady?" I said.

"Right," my mom said. "I saw her at yoga and she told me her daughter is going to be in your class. She's new this year but I told Rhonda that you 3 would show her around."

"Sure," I said.

"What's the daughter's name?" Jonique asked.

"Rhonda calls her Doll but I'm pretty sure that's not her real name," my mom said.

"What's she like?" Melonhead asked.

"I only met her for a minute but I think you'll like her. When I asked Rhonda about her she said, "Doll is so sweet she makes sugar seem sour."

"That's one mother's opinion," Pop said.

"True," my mom said. "But she seemed like a nice kid."

"What does she look like?" Jonique asked.

"She's a pretty girl with blond braids and I

know at least one thing you have in common," my mom said.

"What?" I asked her.

"She was wearing a Gimp key chain necklace that's like the one you made, but not as nice, of course," my mom said.

"Was it pink and white?" Melonhead said.

"I think it was," my mom said.

"Is Rhonda divorced?" I asked her.

"As a matter of fact, she is," my mom said.

"Say it isn't so," Pop said.

"Say it isn't Ashley," I said.

"Say you're not friends with an insect," my dad said because he didn't get that the M.O.T.H.s are actually moms.

"I can't believe I never figured that out," my mom said.

"I can't believe it either," I said.

Jonique was too flabbergasted to talk and all Melonhead could do was howl until we got to Jimmy T's. Then he said, "It's going to take a lot of shakes and burgers to get me over this news."

"We'd better get the works," Pop told him.

"I wish all my customers were such big spenders," Mrs. T said.

"We're living large today," Pop said. "And we're recovering from an unfortunate shock."

"Take the big booth," Mrs. T said. "And tell me what you're drinking."

My dad got a vanilla egg cream which is actually a soda with no eggs in it, thank goodness, and my mom got a chocolate malt. Madam had Red Zinger tea and Melonhead wanted a root beer float. "What can I get you?" she asked Pop.

"Ginger ale," he said. "And 2 lemonades for these 2 girls."

"No problem. We've got lemons today," Mrs. T said.

I pointed to Melonhead and just to be hilarious I said, "And we've got Melon!"

That made me think about the day she said No lemons, no melon. "Pop, may I use your pen?" I asked.

I wrote on a paper napkin and then I could not stop laughing which made everybody look at me including Mrs. T who had come back with our drinks.

"Remember back in the beginning of the summer when you said, 'No lemons, no Melon?' " I asked her.

"Sure," she said.

"Did you know it was a palindrome?" I asked her.

"I had no idea," she said.

August 30

Here's what's unbelievable to me: Out of 92 days only one is left.

Here's another thing: After all of that counting down, my birthday adventure is over and my dad is back in Ann Arbor and I am missing him again. Last night on the phone, he told me, "We both start school on the same day."

"Yes, but you don't have a P-U girl named Ashley in your class," I said.

"I'll bet I have at least one kid just like her," my dad said.

"I cannot believe there are more," I said. "How do you handle a kid like her?"

"I study the situation and come up with a plan," he said.

"I'm big on plans," I said.

Starting tomorrow, I'm going to study the Ashley situation.

Pals for my Pal

noon

radar

race car

lol

pip

wow

dud

go dog

a Toyota

About the Author

Katy Kelly has a lot in common with Lucy Rose. She has red cowgirl boots, a flair for Gimp, a way with words, and is absolutely wild for apricots. Katy Kelly lives with her husband, two daughters, and one dog in Washington, D.C., where she is a senior editor at *U.S. News & World Report*.